Other books by Rick Cleland

Working for KBR in Iraq - An Exercise of Frustration

"GOTCHA"

Al Qaeda Strikes Again

A Novel

By: Rick D. Cleland

www.trafford.com

North America & international
toll-free: 1 888 232 4444 (USA & Canada)
phone: 250 383 6864 ♦ fax: 812 355 4082

THE FATEFUL MEETING

Charles Martin "Marty" Stabler graduated from College with a BA in History and went straight to Marine Corps Officer Candidates' School at Quantico, Virginia, where he received his Commission as a Second Lieutenant. From there, it was a short drive across Interstate 95 to The Basic School for 15 weeks of intensive training for Second Lieutenants. Marty wanted flight training at Naval Air Station, Pensacola, Florida to join the air component of the Marine Corps Air-Ground assault forces, but all would-be pilots were going straight into the helicopter "pipeline" and he wanted to fly jet fighters. Marty decided to go to the Army's Artillery School to become what is known as a "cannon cocker". It was at this time that Ms "career" took a dramatic turn. While at Basic School, he was selected to be a Marine Officer escort for one of the many young ladies taking part in Washington's Annual Cherry Blossom Festival. He was assigned to escort an absolutely gorgeous young lass who had marriage on her mind. Second Lieutenant Charles Martin Stabler did not. Marriage would wait if he considered it at all. For the foreseeable future, Marty Stabler was "married to the Marine Corps", remembering the immortal words of one of his Instructor Gunnery Sergeants, "if the Marine Corps wanted you to have a wife, it would have issued you one". However, during the course of his escort duties, he was introduced to the lady's father and then, through him, to several Congressmen. One was a member of the Senate Intelligence Committee. He gave Lieutenant Stabler his "Official" card with instructions to pass it on to his Commanding Officer ASAP and took one of Marty Stabler's newly-minted "official USMC calling cards" (all Marine Officers are required to have them as part of their "Table of Equipment" or T/E, upon commissioning). Come Monday morning, Charles Martin Stabler's life and Marine Corps career, would take a dramatic turn - for the better (or so he thought at the time).

Come Monday morning, Marty was taken out of "morning formation" and ordered to report to the Commanding Officer of The Basic School, a Colonel. Marty was to report for work as Military Aide to the Chairman of the Senate Intelligence Committee. He was summarily promoted to First Lieutenant and placed on "fast-track" status for Captain. He would be billeted at Anacostia Naval Air Station, across the Anacostia River from Washington and his Permanent Change of Station (PCS) Orders would so indicate. He was "summarily promoted to Captain and again placed on the "fast track", this time to Major. He would need that as a "cover" to avoid suspicion. At the Senator's request, Marty was now assigned as a Defense Intelligence Analyst and given the necessary Security Clearances. He STILL didn't know what the hell it was that he was supposed to be doing other than reporting directly to the Chairman of the Senate Intelligence Committee. He would not be completing The Basic School, a move that would haunt him for the rest of his life, although he didn't know it at the time.

"Snapping In" – Getting Acclimated

Marty Stabler's job was so loosely defined that it was really self-defined. He would have very limited contact with the Senator who had hired him, the other members of the Senate Intelligence Committee, or the Committee Staff. His "position" was not to be "politicized" and any contact initiated by anyone even remotely connected with the Committee, was to be immediately reported to the Chairman who had hired him. He had thoughts of becoming another Ollie North, the Marine Lieutenant Colonel recruited by President Ronald Reagan to perform clandestine Operations in what became known as "trading arms for hostages" in the IRAN-CONTRA SCANDAL. The Congress has specifically prohibited the President from trading arms for hostages in order to effect the release of those Americans taken hostage in the Iranian takeover of the US Embassy in Tehran by Islamic fundamentalists following the fall of the Shah of Iran. Marine Lieutenant Colonel Lawrence Oliver "Ollie" North, operating clandestinely, had carried out the mission of the President in defiance of Congress. Once exposed by the US Media, it damned near caused the impeachment of President Reagan and almost cost Ollie North his Marine Corps retirement pay. In the end, Congress decided to give President Reagan a "pass" on his transgressions and defiance and decided that Lt.Col. North should not be penalized for blindly following the orders of his Commander-in-Chief in accordance with his training.

Marty Stabler decided that he would continue on his present course, knowing no more than he did about his job, what he was expected to do, and the results that were expected therefrom. Marty decided that there was a puzzle to be assembled by him, the pieces of which he had to find and determine if they were a part of the puzzle or a needless diversion from completing the puzzle. He KNEW this much about his job - he had to find out what signals there had been that "9/11" was going to happen, and who was responsible for either ignoring those signals or, more importantly, failing to act on shreds of information that could have led to the completion of the greater picture which WOULD have led to ACTUAL DETERRENCE of that tragic and fatal event. It was not a particularly hard task if you continued to reduce each piece of information to "its lowest common denominator", while ignoring or tossing aside absolutely nothing. He dearly wished that he could ask for the advice of three people - any Marine Gunnery Sergeant, First Sergeant, and Master Sergeant. However, he was reminded of the words of his Sergeant in Officer Candidate School, to wit: "IF you become a Second Lieutenant of Marines, you will be on your own. I will not be there to consult or give you advice or guide you. Learn your lessons well here as we do our best to prepare you to provide your own leadership to those Enlisted Marines whose lives, literally, will depend on the decisions you, alone, must and WILL make. Screw up and they go to one of three places - the nearest medical aid station, the nearest Naval Hospital, or Graves Registration."

Marty was now a Captain and a Major-selectee, meaning that it was just a matter of time before his "Warrant for Promotion" caught up with him and he would "officially" wear the gold leaves of a Major in the Marine Corps. His Official Identification Card showed him as a Federal Agent assigned to the Department of the Treasury along with his Federal Permit to carry a concealed weapon. Where to begin looking for clues that had either been overlooked or discounted as coming from unknown and unverified sources? He decided to begin by visiting Field offices of the FBI, ATF (Alcohol, Tobacco and firearms), and the Immigration and Naturalization Service. He began by checking their incoming telephone logs, telephone answering machines, and e-Mails. He knew that often the best leads came from casual sightings of ordinary citizens. Who had seen suspicious activity and where? He quickly found that even given the telephone numbers of the callers, few calls received were returned. This was a common theme of Federal Investigative Offices nationwide. Their Agents were more interested in "shootouts at the OK Corral" in a Wal-Mart parking lot, than in using all of the toots of standard investigation common to police walking street beats and Detectives following leads in pursuit of criminals. Once Agents received their badges and ID Cards from Treasury, FBI, ATF, INS,CIA, they were "off to the races" to either "shoot 'em", or "collar and cuff'em". They took their job for the excitement and authority and power that came with it, rather than the honest and dogged pursuit of justice that would stand up to a jury trial with evidence legally obtained and properly presented before the presiding Judge. It all began to sicken Marty who had a marked disdain for abuse of power. His Marine Corps training kept his emotions in check while he continued doing his job.

He decided to travel to Oklahoma and Texas, for a close-up "look see" Why? He wanted to see how the investigation of the bombing of the Alfred Murrah Federal Building was handled by the FBI. Then on to Dallas and Fort Worth to see how those Offices of the FBI had handled foreign Nationals going to and from Mexico and points South in Central and South America. He barely got to show his credentials at the Dallas FBI Office when the Agent-in-Charge made a phone call to someone and within fifteen minutes he was handed a Restraining Order barring him from the Office. It was signed by a Federal District Court Judge He soon found out that the call had been made to a retired FBI Agent who was a sort of "Mother Hen" over the Dallas Office and was well-connected, politically. Now a Marine Major, Marty made a note in his Diary, "Investigation of Dallas FBI Office blocked by Federal Court Order. Officer-in-Charge uncooperative. Departed without incident". Now he was on to the Fort Worth FBI Office. It was here that the FBI had arrested an Islamic Medical Doctor who had attempted to leave by train shortly after the Oklahoma City bombing. It had been assumed that the OKC bombing was the work of Islamic terrorists and the good Doctor had fit the "profile" and was, therefore, "detained" for questioning. He was interrogated at great length, but was never formally charged with any violation of the law. His "detention" lasted just long enough for him to miss his train and mess up all of his subsequent travel plans. No formal apology was ever issued to him for his delay in transit. Marty, with only a couple of Law School classes at night, was becoming quite concerned about the obvious violations of the Constitutional Civil Rights of those being detained under the practice of "profiling". At what point might his investigation cause him to alert the US Department of Justice's Civil Rights Division ? He dismissed his concern since, while legitimate, it was outside of the scope of his mission. It would be up to the "detainees" to file their own lawsuits in defense of their own Civil Rights.

In the Fort Worth Office of the FBI, he was warmly received and given full access. He found only several incoming phone calls that were not logged-in, even at the specific request of the caller. They all pertained to personal theories behind the OKC bombing. He told the Agent-in Charge to just be more diligent in following up on all incoming telephone calls. He said, "you just never know when you'll get a tiny shred of information, which, when added to other tiny shreds information, completes the puzzle that alerts us all to a crime about to be committed." He left the Office encouraged that they had gotten his message. At least they had not "stonewalled" him as the Dallas office had.

He decided to make a trip overseas, to Iraq. He needed to follow-up on the findings, or more appropriately, the lack thereof, of Marine General Tony Zinni. President Bush had dispatched the Marine three-star General to get proof of Saddam's presumed stockpile of WMDs which had eluded the United Nations Chief Investigator, Hans Biix, who had been temporarily denied access to several of Saddam's Presidential Palaces just long enough for the Iraqis to have time to perform coverups, as, or if necessary. General Zinni, who had access to all American, Allied, and NATO intelligence, had found nothing new. He had reported back to the President that there were no WMDs to be found and probably never were. President Bush was not happy with General Zinni's findings and informed the General to "put in your request for retirement with over 30 years of Honorable Service". Marty would go to Iraq following an extremely low-profile approach. However, he needed a "cover" and it was arranged for him to be an "employee" of Blackhawk Services, Inc. They had the US Government Contract to provide "protective services" for any Civilians, working under US Government Contract, in Iraq. Blackhawk's Modus Operandi was to "shoot first and ask questions later", or at least that was the public's perception of their Operations.

Marty didn't bother to check-in with the CPA (Coalition Provisional Authority) and didn't even enter the "Green Zone" initially. He had been given enough contacts with the Tribal Leaders in Baghdad and had been assigned an Interpreter. He had somewhat "grown-out" his standard Marine Corps "high and tight" haircut and had grown a neatly-trimmed dark brown moustache. He hired a 'local" to drive him to Mosul, up the road from Tikrit. He wanted to know the relationship between the Kurds of Mosul and the Turks occupying their common border with Iraq. However, before departing Baghdad, he just had to visit the Green Zone. He showed his American Passport to the Guard at Saddam's Primary Presidential Palace in Baghdad - a huge and ornate structure of all-marble construction. The Guard was Tibetan, about feet five inches tall and very stocky. The guard stared straight ahead as Marty flipped open his Passport. The Tibetan showed no interest in looking at it. Marty placed it straight in front of the Tibetan's eyes and received a slight grin which almost appeared to literally crack the skin of his olive, round, Asian face. The Tibetan quickly flipped his rifle, which had been at "parade rest" from his right side to his left side, thereby freeing up his right hand to reach out and grab the large handle of the huge wooden door and pull the door open for Marty to pass through. Once inside, it was obvious that the US Army was in total control here. He saw nothing but Field Grade Officers - mostly Majors and Lieutenant Colonels and there was a gob of them. Where the hell are all of the Lieutenants and Captains, Marty thought to himself? He finally asked someone. He was told that all Offices in the Main Presidential Palace were occupied by Senior Army Officers, Diplomats of almost every Country in the UN, and Iraqi Cabinet Members. He had arrived at noon chow time. It was assumed that he wanted to eat lunch, so he was gently nudged onto the end of the chow line He soon came upon a table full of small bottles of a clear fluid. An Iraqi waiter motioned to him to stretch out his hands, palms up. Some of the clear liquid was squeezed onto both of his hands. It had a scent of ammonia to it. It was hand sanitizer and he was to rub it into both of his hands by vigorously rubbing his hands together. He then entered the buffet line where the food was plentiful and attractively displayed and presented to each diner. He was one of the last to receive actual ceramic salad and main serving plates. All others received plastic plates and utensils. He had a choice of baked chicken or fish. Marty selected the chicken, although he could have received both, had he indicated his desire. He was shown to a large upright cooler for his choice of beverage, in pint cardboard containers. There was milk, strawberry milk, and chocolate milk and you could take as many containers as you wished. All of it was imported from Denmark or Sweden. He found himself a seat at a banquet table covered by a white table cloth and metal folding chairs. He ate rather quickly in order to avoid questions about who he was, in his civilian attire. He left nothing uneaten on his plate except a few "cleaned" chicken bones, so he scraped the bones into a large trash can and added his plate to the stack of plates on the adjacent table. He went on a quick tour of the Palace and almost everywhere was a "haji" (pronounced HAH-GEE -a makeshift store atop a table with a glass-enclosed showcase). These were Iraqi Vendors, selling their wares for cash USD (US Dollars, as different from Kuwaiti Dollars). The most prevalent merchandise was French and British perfumes, wristwatches, knives, and tobacco. Genuine Cuban cigars sold for one Dollar each. "Generic" French and British cigarettes (similar to Marlboro, Marty was told) sold for three to four dollars a carton. No liquor or liquers was available.

Marty was anxious to see the effects of the "shock and awe" that President Bush had promised would rain down on Baghdad from the Tomahawk Cruise Missiles that had been fired from US ships in the Persian Gulf and UK submarines in the Red Sea. He walked to the Communications Building from which Saddam was to have Command and Control of his Defense Forces, most notably, his highly-touted Republican Guard, during the initial invasion of US forces. He entered the multi-storied concrete building and immediately had to walk around and duck debris, ductwork, and myriad hanging cables. He came upon a room which had been full of mainframe computers. It was a total shambles. Just down the hall was a window to the outside. It had been blown-out by a Cruise missile that had been targeted for the computer room. Absolutely amazing, Marty mused to himself. Such accuracy! An Iraqi came up to Marty and seeing the expression on his face, added that the missile had actually flown around a lamppost on the corner of the building and still entered the window at a right angle. Marty wondered how many digits were required for the actual target coordinates? He later leaned that there were no coordinates used. A secret DOD satellite had fed a photo-image to the launch ship which had been digitally encoded into the guidance system of the Cruise Missile. That still didn't explain how the hell a twenty-foot missile could make a right-angle turn into a window from about thirty feet. The answer was that the missile cannot. It flew around the light pole, flew out and up about 100 feet, then flew in a tight turn to the left, leveled-out at about 100 feet directly in front of the window and then flew straight into the window. That's how !

Marty finished his sight-seeing and returned to his quarters. He had taken a room at the Hotel Al Rasheed on the Tigris Rive and about a mile or so from the Green Zone. The Hotel was a high rise structure of concrete and glass, It where most journalists and buninessmen stayed if they were looking for lucrative contracts with Kellogg Brown & Root or one of the many other Contractors who did business with the Iraqis through the Coalition Provisional Authority. Most were Syrian, Jordanian, or Egyptian. At any given time, there would be half a dozen of them, each of medium height, athletic build, and impeccably groomed, wearing a lightweight fabric suit. Marty wondered why they almost always stood up and kept their jackets fully buttoned. He soon found out why when one of them finally sat down in one of the many upholstered chairs in the ornate lobby. He had an Israeli-made Uzi submachine gun in a shoulder holster and what looked like a Colt Python 357 revolver in a clip-on holster on his belt. Smoking was permitted in the Lobby and free liter bottles of water lined up on the Registration Desk counter. Koreans were in charge of all Hotel Security and were omnipresent. Marty had a good night of sleep except for the occasional "ping" of small pieces of concrete being chipped off the side of the hotel by snipers shooting at maximum range from the other side of the nearby Tigris river.

He was to join an Army Convoy at 0800 for Tikrit. He would find out at 0800 that, unlike the Marine Corps, when the Array scheduled a convoy to leave at 0800, it would actually be more like 0930 or later. He piled his one suitcase and backpack into the rear of an SUV and took a seat behind the driver. A soldier walked up to the driver of the SUV and instructed him to step out. There was a meeting of all convoy drivers with the Leader in the lead Hummer. The driver turned to Marty and, appearing somewhat surprised and shaken, asked Marty to take over as the driver and attend the meeting. Marty did so The Convoy Leader explained the rules of the Convoy to all drivers. There was the lead Hummer and then three SUVs, then another Hummer and another three SUVs, and so on up to the last vehicle which was another Hummer, Only the lead Hummer had an automatic weapon top-mounted, which was essentially an M60 machine gun firing 7.62

mm NATO ammunition - each "round" about as big in circumference as a dime and roughly three inches long. It was a "crew-served" weapon using "linked" ammunition. The links were metal clips which linked one round to the next one for rapid fire. As each round approached the weapon's firing chamber (or breech), a final turn of the round would strip away the metal clip and the bolt going forward would force the round into the firing chamber. The belted ammo went from the roof gunner directly to a steel ammo can between the legs of the Assistant Gunner sitting in the back seat. The steel can contained 500 rounds of ammunition- On full automatic (trigger pulled back and HELD back by the Gunner), the clips almost literally rained down on the feet of the Assistant Gunner in the back. He would constantly shake them off his boots and kick them off to the side onto the floor of the Hummer. If and when the floor became full of clips, he'd grab handfuls of them and toss them out the window. The brass shell casings from the spent bullets extracted from the firing chamber went every which way until gravity finally took them wherever. Back to the briefing. The driver was never to get closer than about 30 feet to the vehicle in front of him and drop back no further than 100 feet. Under no circumstances was any vehicle to permit another vehicle to cross through the Convoy or enter into it. When they slowed to pass through a town, they were to permit no person, regardless of gender or age to attempt to cross the street between vehicles. If anyone attempted to do so, the driver was to run them over, pure and simple, Marty said, somewhat audibly, though not loudly, "yeah, right. Just run them over and kill them dead, right there, in the middle of the street." The Convoy Leader must have heard him and addressed Marty directly and personally. "You got a problem with that, Charlie Brown?" The comment caught Marty off guard and flustered him for a brief moment. "Well, lemme tell ya somethin' right here and now, Buster. This ain't the States. There ain't no Law here at all. I'm the fucking law - I'm the big, bad-assed Sheriff and when I tell you to kill, you damned well better kill or I'll kill YOU myself. I won't waste a bullet on your sorry ass. One quick stroke across your throat with this here Army hunting knife and we get to play soccer with your head. NOW, do I make myself purrfekly clear, Bozo?" The Marine in Marty wanted to take this wiseass apart at the seams and leave him for the buzzards, BUT, this was neither the time nor the place for a flash of "a Marine Grunt's temper". His reply was a comical "yowser, Mister Master - you de boss, Mister Master, sir" along with the kind of salute Dick Clark used to sign off on his weekly American Bandstand back in the 1960s. For a second, Marty wondered if the Soldier on the roof weapon knew to fire in bursts limited to about five rounds each to avoid the buildup of heat which WILL cause the barrel to turn first, visibly red hot and then white hot until the steel barrel literally sags and causes first a jam and then the heat buildup becomes so intense that it causes the brass shell casing of the round in the firing chamber to expand and "weld" itself to the steel wall of the firing chamber to the point where extraction of the round in the chamber is impossible and the weapon becomes totally useless.

Marty returned to his assigned SUV and took his seat behind the steering wheel and buckled his seatbelt. One last piece of information Marty had from his briefing by the Convoy Leader. He shared it with his passengers. IF they should be ambushed, the Hummers will return fire just long enough to permit all civilian vehicles to pull out of the Convoy and "floor the gas" for about five miles up the road where they were to pull to the side of the road and wait until the Hummers finished their work and joined them to continue the trip. "Got that, everybody?" All heads nodded. "Good, then let's get this show on the road and get the Hell out of Dodge." By now it was 10:30 AM and it was starting to get hot. The tank of the SUV was full of gas and the air conditioner worked. All of the main roads around the Green Zone had "T-walls" in place of what would be double yellow or white lanes. T-walls were made of concrete loaded with rebar and about ten feet high. They were called T-walls because if you looked at them from the side, they looked like an inverted letter "T". At the top of each were two pieces of rebar, each bent into the shape of a U and imbedded into the concrete- These were used for the hooks of large, truck-mounted cranes to pick them up and move them. They were transported on flat-bed trucks in two rows of three walls each. On demand, they could be tilted out to form a "breech in the wall" for traffic to pass through. They soon came upon one such opening and Marty maneuvered through it. Once on the other side of the wall, they quickly sped up as they were leaving

They were on a four-lane divided highway with modest, cinder-block houses of maybe 500 to 700 square feet on each side of the road, set back maybe 100 feet. Mile after mile, the side of the road was littered with relics of wars past - all armaments of one type or another. Everything from a burned-out Russian or German tank, to German anti-aircraft guns. Aside from the charring from where they had been hit and burned, the metal, mostly steel, was remarkably intact. Marty later found out that this was due to a combination of the heat in Iraq and the low humidity. He also found out that it had been estimated that if you took all of this "wartime debris" and stacked it level-full to the roof of the Texas Stadium or Yankee Stadium, or any similar ballpark, and did so every day for an entire year, and blew it all up, you STILL would not get rid of it all.

About half an hour out of Baghdad, the Convoy pulled to the side of the road. All drivers "dismounted" and walked to the lead Hummer. There had been a change of plans and the Convoy would terminate at Camp Anaconda, about twenty miles up the road and five miles to the east. Camp Anaconda had been Saddam's Main Air Base, known as Al Assad. It was huge and sprawling, taking in maybe a couple of thousand acres or more. It had a concrete runway of 10,000 feet or more and could easily land a C-141, C-5, or B-52. Marty would spend the night there and worry about transport to the North to Tikrit in the morning. Since he was posing as a civilian "contract employee", he cast his lot for the night at the small compound for Kellogg, Brown & Root (known to the Army, DOD and DOS, as simply, "KBR"). Goddammit if there weren't T-walls EVERYWHERE. It was only about a one acre compound and yet there must have been a hundred of those damned monstrosities everywhere he looked. THAT, plus the solid foot of crushed rock you had to walk on everywhere you went, made foot travel quite an ordeal.

It was like trying to walk on a very sandy beach in boots - two feet forward, slide back one foot. AND, you could get absolutely no traction underfoot. The best was yet to come - having to take a pee at "oh-dark-thirty" in a horrible-smelling Porta Potty that was a hundred feet away from your tent, requiring you to navigate your way around a maze of T-walls, while walking with flip-flops atop the foot of crushed rock with only the light of a flashlight, the beam of which went everywhere when you stumbled with each step on the crushed rock shifting as you placed your weight on it. Constantly drinking bottled water really cleaned out your kidneys and bladder and did so VERY frequently during the day and night. After the second trip to the Porta Potty, Marty opted for "field expediency", to wit: just open the end tent flap, turn to your left, whip it out, pee, put it back where it came from, and hit the rack again. Problem solved !

Marty was finished relying on the US Army for much of anything. However, he was forced to learn some Army "lingo". In order to eat something besides MREs, you did not go to a Mess Hall. The Army called it a "D-FAC" (pronounced "DeeFack" and stood for Dining Facility). There were no Mess Kits or metal trays. They used flat fiberglass trays to hold the heavy plastic plates for the food - large one for the entree, small ones for salad and dessert. When you were finished eating, you tilted the tray over a large plastic trash can and just kind of banged the tray against the trash can lined with a black plastic bag until everything fell off the tray and into the can. When the liner was full, it was tied-ff, jerked out of the can, tossed off to the side, and replaced with a new liner. Local Iraqis were used for labor, especially working freshly-poured concrete. Marty was in line for chow at the D-Fac when a loud horn suddenly sounded. Marty thought it was a siren for "incoming" (hostile fire) and started for the nearest place for cover. He damned near kicked an Iraqi in the ribs. The horn was a "call to Prayer", sounded from the nearest Mosque and all Iraqis "dropped like a rock" after whipping out a small rug from somewhere on their body. They knelt down on it and then bowed toward Mecca and did this three times in the space of about five minutes. During this time, they were totally oblivious to anything or anybody around them. Then they got back on their feet and went back to work.

Marty sought out a Soldier with a lot of stripes on the upper arm. That person would probably be able to give him some travel information, or at least point him in the right direction. The first such person he saw was a female. He asked her rank and she replied "Command Sergeant-Major". That made her roughly equivalent to a Marine Sergeant-Major, as opposed to a Marine Master Gunnery Sergeant. The "Command" part of her title made the difference since she was an "Operations-type" versus an "Administrative-type", at least according to the Army. She did give him the name of Major who might be able to help him with his transportation needs.

He had taken about all the "jerking around" he was going to tolerate from the Army (if they only knew that he was a Marine Captain and who he reported to. That's IT - suddenly he had the answer to put an end to all the crap). He had his Treasury H) with him and when he found the Army Major, he would say that he reported directly to a Rear Admiral at Langley and was headed to Tikrit to perform an Audit. That should get him some cooperation. If there was anything the Military feared more than an Audit or a formal investigation under the jurisdiction of the UCMJ (Uniform Code of military Justice), it was someone from Langley (Virginia - the Home Office of the Central Intelligence Agency). Marty finally found the Major and told him that he was fed up with Convoys and wanted the next flight of any kind, headed to Tikrit. Ideally, he wanted a seat on a C&C (Command and Control) helo, probably a UH-1E, but he'd settle for a seat on a C-130 (which could land on a SATS -Short Airstrip for Tactical Support- Base and take-off again with J ATO (jet-assisted take-off) bottles temporarily bolted on to the body of the

"Here" (the C-130 is a four-engine prop-driven cargo and aerial refueling aircraft known as a "Hercules'1, for its airlift capabilities. It is incredibly aerodynamic and can stay aloft at close to stall-out speed (around 160 MPH of ground speed). Anyway, the Major would see what he could arrange and told Marty to "hang loose and ready to roll on short notice". Marty had picked up the new title of "Federal Agent", which suited him just fine since it afforded him newfound respect and, to some degree, preferential treatment by the Army. He hopped in the back of the Major's jeep for the short ride to the helo landing pad where they waited for Marty's "hop" to Tikrit. Soon, Marty could hear the "wop-wop-wop" of the approaching helo. It came into the pad "tactically" - low, fast, ass-heavy (tail down), roughly 30 degrees from horizontal, leveled-off fast at about 30 feet, then dropped again, ass-heavy until both skids hit the landing pad with an audible crunch. Marty hopped aboard and sat directly behind the passenger who was a Colonel -a Brigade Commander, the Colonel made a circling-motion with his right index finger held above his head. The pilot increased engine RPMs to full throttle, increased torque on the rotor blades and made a hard left turn away from the landing pad. Marty was finally headed for Tikrit to begin his fact-finding mission for his boss, the Senator. Marty's helo was quickly "shadowed" by an Army Blackhawk helicopter bristling with armaments. Through his headset, Marty heard his pilot use the Blackhawk pilot's call sign of "Blackwidow" - an apparent reference to the deadly spider. The Crew Chief told Marty the Blackwidow was a female Army Captain who could make the Blackhawk "dance" - she's all business - no bullshit and can fly that bird straight up your ass and make you fart. They landed at Tikrit and were met by an Army Colonel. He asked, "is there a Mr. Stabler aboard?" Marty answered, "yes, that's me, sir". "Well dismount and follow me in my jeep." The jeep took Marty to the Colonel's CP (Command Post). Once there, the Colonel told Marty, "I don't know what this is all about, young man, but I've been ordered by the Commanding Officer of Third MEF (Marine Expeditionary Force), to promote you to the rank of Major in the Marine Corps and I have been given a Uniform with your gold leaves already on the collar which you are to put on immediately. I am then to arrange your immediate transport to Mosul, to our North. You will be taken in my personal Command and Control bird and you will depart immediately. The bird is already fired-up for you and is waiting to lift-off. Assuming you are in agreement, that is all. Dismissed." Marty asked the Colonel, "I had arranged motor transport provided by one of the local tribal chiefs, to Mosul. What am I to do about that? Is there any way I can cancel that? "Major, I am aware of that and I have already taken care of that. You have your instructions, now carry them out before the hospitality of the Army toward the Marine Corps gets any thinner. Now, do me a favor, Major, and get the hell out of here and get you ass to Mosul to do whatever the hell third MEF wants you to do. I do not take kindly to having to carry out the orders of Marine Corps Generals. They have their agendas and I have mine and the two rarely mix well. Now, get the hell out of my CP."

THE WORLD OF INTERNATIONAL INTRIGUE

The newly-promoted Maj or Martin Stabler had to find a way to get rid of his Marine Uniform and Major's Gold Oak Leaves and Pronto. He told the helo pilot to keep the engine "hot" on the Command and Control "bird" while he made a fast trip to a nearby Porta-Potty. He found one, emptied his bladder and changed back into his civilian clothes, tucking his uniform, neatly folded, under his arm. after removing the pinned-on Major's rank and putting the pair of gold leaves, no bigger than about the size if a dime, into his trouser pocket. He dropped the desert-cammy blouse (shirt) and trousers into a trash can he passed on the way back to the helo. He was thankful that he didn't have to "ditch" an Army uniform, since the Major's "leaves" would have been sewn on to the lapel and were as big as a half-dollar. He never did understand that about the Army. Officers' rank insignia were so large - Four-Star Generals had the stars going around their collar almost to the back of their neck. Marines always used pinned-on Officers' rank insignia and even the Commandant's four small silver stars were only about 2 1/2 inches long. Ah, well, interesting - and life goes on just as before.

The helo ride to Mosul was, thankfully, uneventful. Marty put on the spare headset and listened to the pilot flying the helo - she was all-business and no bull shit. She made a near-perfect landing with the skids instead of wheels. Marty removed the headset and deplaned, spinning around to "pop the pilot a salute" along with a "thumbs-up". She flipped a switch to power the "psy-ops" (psychological operations) bullhorn, externally mounted on the helo, and said simply, "enjoyed your company, Sir, Have a great day in Mosul". She then changed the torque on the helo's blades to give them more "bite" into the wind, quickly lifted off about three feet, swung the tail around into the wind (of which there wasn't much on this day), pitched the whole helo into a wicked "angle of attack" into the wind, and shot skyward like being shot out of a cannon.

Marty didn't bother to check in with the CPA (Coalition Provisional Authority) American Colonel in charge of the Mosul Area of Operations, since he was really on a Covert fact-finding Mission for the Chairman of the Senate Intelligence Committee. He checked into a local Hotel and "put-out-the- word" that he needed to contact several of the local Kurdish "tribal leaders". He would be available in the hotel coffee shop and "identifiable" as the Westerner smoking a walerpipe. It wasn't long before a man approached him and inquired as to whether he might be the American Mr. Stabler. Marty nodded, affirmatively, stood up, and with a gesture of his hand, invited the inquisitor to join him at the table. The man did so, while politely refusing to partake of the waterpipe. That gave Marry a good excuse to end HIS use of the pipe, since the tobacco was Turkish, very pure and quite strong. His guest said something in Arabic to the waiter and soon two small, ceramic cups were served, each containing a very dark coffee liquer. Marty didn't know whether to try to sip the liquid or just dip his tongue into it which appeared to be a quantity of about three ounces. Marty was looking around for maybe some bottled water for a "chaser", when his guest raised his cup, indicated he he wanted to make a toast in friendship, clinked his cup with his host and summarily gulped-down the contents of the cup. He then swirled Ms tongue around the inside of the small cup to savor the remaining residue. "Damn" thought Marty, to himself- "this beats the hell out of a shot and a beer at the Dirty Shame stag bar at Cherry Point Marine Air Station in North Carolina. His guest excused himself to go make a telephone call to invite another person to join them. Marty had no idea what to expect.

Soon the other person appeared and joined them. There had been an unexpected change in plans. Something had occurred, very recently, which would have a "ripple effect" from Mosul to Tikrit, to Baghdad, to Houston in the United States. It had been known, for some time, hi covert circles, that the Israelis had an "Operative" in northern Iraq. He was an Agent of the Moussad, the Israeli Intelligence Service, carrying dual Passports as both an Israeli and American. The Israelis were very concerned both about a known Iranian nuclear reactor and its "accelerated" program to enrich uranium to "weapons grade".

Marty knew that it takes several hundred centrifuges to enrich enough uranium to produce even one small bomb. Western Intelligence sources had information that the Iranians would soon have 500 such centrifuges. They use "cetri-petal" (inward) force to condense metals into "critical mass" which is how a one-inch cube of metal can be made so dense that it has to be handled with special equipment. Thus, Albert Einstein's formula of "E=MC2" or "Energy equals Mass, multiplied by fissionable material, squared.. Einstein (and later J. Robert Oppenheimer, Originator of the Code-named "Manhattan Project" whose bomb ended the Japanese Empire in World War II), correctly reasoned that if you could condense certain metals to be dense enough, and then bombard the mass uniformly, sequentially, from all sides, extremely rapidly. The atoms of the condensed metal would react by expanding extremely rapidly and violently, giving off intense heat along with high, very hot winds, and, of course, varying degrees of radiation which causes body-cell breakdown. The large number of centrifuges were needed because each one was capable of reducing the size of the metal to be condensed by only the size of a human hair per month. When you start with a volume the size of a basketball and end up with a volume the size of a large olive - all of it solid metal, it takes a lot of time. The CIA, the Brits, the French, the Chinese, and the Israelies all had different estimates of how far along in the progress toward a detonatable AND deliverable nuclear weapon the Iranians really were. The Israelis were, as usual, the most reliable and formidable of all of the Intelligence Agencies. Their famous raid on the airliner hijacked to Entebbe, resulting in no casualties, was a model for how to successfully deal with hijackers. Five dead gunmen, no other casualties.

The Israeli Moussad Agent had been trying to get a feel for two separate situations - one, how close were the Kurds in southern Turkey to allying with the Kurds in the Mosul area of northern Iraq. If the International Coalition could provide both security and stability to the Mosul area, would the two Kurdish groups unite to form a Sovereign Nation, independent of both Turkey and Iraq ? They would, no doubt, request immediate diplomatic recognition from both the United Nations and the United States. Both Entities would have little choice but to grant the desired recognition. That would really complicate the "map" of the entire region. Kurds would then have full control of the vast oil fields of northern Iraq, receiving enough "petro-dollars" to become another Kuwait or Qatar. They could immediately afford all of the Armaments they needed to protect their new-found independence and "diplomatic recognition of 'Kurdistan' as a legitimate political power" in the region. They would be every bit as potent as Israel which had gained its International recognition and sovereignty from the United Nations in 1948 , when it was given its sovereignty over Palestinian land and territory. Although Israel had been a precedent, could Israel now allow the Kurds of Mosul to be the latest Chapter in the precedent ? The Israeli Agent also wanted to find out if the Kurds, who had "allies and brother" tribesmen in the western mountains of Iran, could be counted on to clandestinely and surreptitiously provide intelligence to the Israelies on the progress, if any, being made by Iran to produce a functional, deliverable, nuclear weapon capable of striking Israel ?

Concurrently, "word" was being circulated that the US President was so "pissed" at the Turks for failing to allow US to stockpile war materiel on their territory to support a northern (in addition to a southern) invasion of Iraq, that the US would support a "breakaway" Kurdish Nation-State. The Israelis were trying to determine if it would be better for their interests to have Kurdish tribes supplying them information, or a Sovereign Kurdish Nation. A Nation might have Diplomatic, Military, Economic, and Social issues to deal with, while individual tribal leaders would not. Therefore, the Israeli Intelligence Agent's presence. Well, somehow, that had very recently been compromised. The Moussad Agent had "fallen off the radar" and just disappeared. THAT was what Marty's second guest "for coffee" had come to make known to the American Agent. Marty knew the value of information gained by Agents of its Moussad and so he set about trying to find the Agent. The Agent had gone to Baghdad where he was told, by the CPA to stay in the Al Rasheed Hotel overnight and a car would come for him at first light. Sometime during the night, the Agent had slipped out of the hotel and, again, disappeared. Marty later found that Tel Aviv had instructed him to return to HQ via Houston. The route had been Baghdad to Kuwait to Amsterdam to Detroit to Chicago to Houston' s George Bush International.

Marty was set to go "sniffing" around Mosul a bit more when he got word that the CPA was going to entertain a Congressional Delegation headed by the US Secretary of State and that both Tikrit and Mosul was on their itinerary. That left the possibility that there might a Senator among them who knew his connection to the Chair of the Senate Intel Committee and what he was really doing in Iraq. Marty reminded himself of the expression that "loose lips sink ships". He did not want to be aimlessly floating around Iraq with a bunch of Congressional "yahoos" loose and "on the prowl". Ollie North would never have been discovered if he had not been in the background of some press photos taken in Managua, Nicaragua on a Mission for President Reagan. That was the infamous "arms for hostages" deal he was negotiating with the Contras up against the Sandanistas, in direct violation and defiance of Congress. Reagan had the "cover" of "National Security interest". LtCol North had no such cover and when the verbal bullets started flying from Congressional small-arms fire, it damned near cost the Colonel his Marine Corps Retirement. No - there was no point in Marty hanging around. He would head back to Washington and check in with his Boss.

A SUDDEN CHANGE OF PLANS

It wasn't long before Major Stabler got a call on his GPS telephone. It came from "CMC -Code 1". That meant the Commandant of the Marine Corps, himself.. The text message, sent "in the open" (unencrypted), read "Stabler, Westman, Stevens to report, ASAP, to CG, CLNC. CMC will attend. Use A/C provided by VMGR, Camp Anaconda, for direct flight non-stop, to CPNC. Report in Greens to appropriate USMC standards - out". Marty immediately contacted Westman and Stevens and told them to meet him at Camp Anaconda where the MARLOG Flight manifests passengers. They were to use their USMC IDs to "clear the Main Gate" and ask for an Army Military Police vehicle to take them to the Marine "staging area". The three Marines met up and boarded the C-130 Hercules transport for the Looong flight to Cherry Point which would require two aerial refuelings - one over the Mediterranean and one southwest of Gibraltar, somewhere near the Canary Islands off the northwestern coast of Africa. Roughly six thousand air miles at an average airspeed of about 550-600 MPH (not counting head or tail winds - strong headwinds could slow them to just fast enough to keep them aloft, while strong tail winds could add as much as 200 MPH to their airspeed. It all really depended on the global track of the Airstream at the actual time of flight).

The C-130 landed at Cherry Point Marine Air Station just as the sun was rising in the East. Stepping off the Aircraft, they were met by a Marine Colonel who identified himself as the Chief-of-Staff to the Commanding General of the Second Marine Aircraft Wing. In the interest of time, he would take them in his Staff car to the Navy Hostess House to perform the "four S's -shave, shower, shit, shampoo". He allowed them an hour to do so. hi the interim, he would arrange for their crumpled "Greens" to be ironed and pressed to USMC standards. He then took them to a nearby helo pad where the Commandant's personal helicopter was standing-by for the short flight to Camp

LeJeune where they were to meet with the CG, 2ndMARDIV, and CMC "Actual". They WERE told that they were not in any kind of trouble, but they would have to answer a lot of questions to the satisfaction of the Commandant. At Camp LeJeune, they were taken to the Commanding General's Conference Room where they met THE Commandant. Also in attendance were the Sergeant-Major of the Marine Corps and the Sergeant-Major of the Second Marine Division, since two of the Marines present were Staff Non-Commissioned Officers. The three Marines were shown to seats at the large, wooden, conference table. The Commandant addressed them. "Marines, let's get right down to business. I know that the three of you are on T-A-D Orders with no Expiration Date. I also know that those Orders were issued to you by the Central Intelligence Agency as well as ID Cards for each of you. I know that Sergeants Stevens and Westman became a part of this, Mission (or Endeavor) at the specific request of Major Stabler. He chose you because of your expertise in areas where he needed experience and discipline in order to attempt and accomplish his Mission. It appears to me that he made the correct decision in his choice of you two Enlisted Marines. Your involvement in this Mission came to my attention because probably, at least 100 Members of the Congress received "concerns" from their Constituents. Those concerns had to do with Marines from their Districts who became aware of Major Stabler's rapid rise in Rank from Second Lieutenant to Major in just under two years. Those Marines were concerned with, as Marine Stabler received rapid promotion, were they to be considered to have been "passed over" for promotion, either officially or unofficially? Now, Major, normally I just "blow off" that sort of shit as either disgruntled Marines, or disgruntled parents of possibly unhappy Lieutenants. However, when 100 or more Members of the House, out of a total of about 260 Members, start calling me and my staff, it has a way of getting my attention. I think you can see my problem here. I have, therefore, with the support of the Navy Office of Judge Advocate General, taken the following steps and made the following decisions, retroactively to today. All three of you Marines are under legal Contract to the United States Marine Corps. At no time, during your Contract, are you on any kind of "loan" to any other person or "Entity", to include one or more Members of the Congress. There is no legal standing for anyone outside of the Marine Corps to "borrow you or your service(s)" for any reason whatsoever. YOU ARE SOLELY US MARINE CORPS PROPERTY as a legal form of indentured servitude, under the Constitution. Others may request your services or expertise, but may not do so without the expressed WRITTEN consent of the Commandant of the Marine Corps AND the Secretary of the Navy. Major, I have asked the Secretary of the Navy to have the Vice President, as Presiding officer of the Senate, to inform the Senator who "hired you" that he "exceeded his Authority" in doing so. Your CIA credentials are revoked and the Commanding General of the Second Marine Division will immediately reassign you to a Unit within his Command. Your rank will be First Lieutenant and you will be moved to the top of the Promotion List for Captain to join your fellow Classmates from The Basic School. Master Sergeant Westman will be reunited with the Unit from which he was reassigned to work with Marine Stabler. Gunnery Sergeant Stevens will be reunited with the Unit from which he was reassigned to work with Marine Stabler. That is all for now, Gentlemen. I have scheduled briefings with each of you for tomorrow to learn what you found out in Iraq so that I can pass it along to the Joint Chiefs at our next meeting. That is all, Marines, and this meeting is adjourned. Major Stabler, please remain, since I have some questions for you, alone. We're having pizza for lunch. I can't eat pizza without a cold beer. Will you join me for one? You bet Sir. Great, now I want to know what you found out that Colin Powell and Tony Zinni could not Sir, are we 'off the record', here, sir? Yes, we're off the record. Good, Sir. The steel pipes manufactured by the Germans, allegedly to have sections welded to form the barrel of long-range artillery to deliver deadly chemicals onto Israelis, we never intended to do so. They were to be buried in the ground to form tunnels to move troops from location to another without being detected. Saddam relied solely upon his Scud Missiles to do that job. To strike any part of Israel, the Scuds were at maximum range. However, Saddam reaped a benefit from them, nonetheless. We had Patriot Missile Batteries deployed in Israel. The Patriots were the primary defense against the Scuds. The firing crews of the Patriots had never "fam" fired one in practice. When their radar first acquired a Scud "incoming", they didn't fire a Patriot until they were certain that it would not overfly Israel and land, harmlessly, into the Mediterranean. When the Scud was certain to strike Israel, they launched the Patriot. The net effect was to hit the Scud in its "fat" part as it showed up on the radar and cause the Scud to break up in flight, sending its fragmented parts raining down like hundreds of artillery shells. The effect of the fiery conflagration, from a "psy-ops" point of view, was much more effective than the possible death toll or number of injuries. The Russians supplied NVGs to Saddam, but the technology is crude, with pictures very grainy and targets indistinguishable as mere blobs of varing shades of pink and red. We did find that the Kurds at Mosul knew about movements of the al Quada, but Osama remained very elusive and shadowy. They also knew of the plans of Mohammed Atta and tried to warn the West, but their info was "shrugged off" as unknown, unconfirmed, unconfirmable, and unreliable, since none of their "number" was a confirmed, reliable, informant. The attitude of the anti-Saddamists/Baath Party-ists, was that Ambassador Paul Bremer had his "known" sources of information and neither needed nor welcomed any other. Iraqis had their own problems in the aftermath of the US invasion. The just didn't care about the calamity and destruction of two large buildings on the south end of New York City. Their attitude was, "Sorry it happened, but we have our own problems here - we'll bury our dead - you bury your dead. And life goes on - shit happens ! "Just how did you get involved in all of this, Major?" "Sir, I was at TBS and was asked to escort a young lady at the Cherry Blossom Festival. She turned out to be the daughter of a Senator who was Chairman of the Senate Intelligence Committee. I don't know if his daughter was smitten with me or if I made a very good impression on her father, the Senator. The next thing I knew was that I was talking with a Marine Lieutenant Colonel who was the Military Aide to the Senator. He gave me my assignment, TAD Orders with no Expiration Date, and then sent me to Langely to be briefed on what the Senator wanted me to do, given a CIA Badge and ID and told to be on an aircraft bound for Germany in a few days." "Major, who signed your TAD Orders?" "The Senator's Aide did, sir". "Did you question his authority to do so?" "Sir, I was still a Second Lieutenant assigned to TBS. At that Pay Grade, newly-Commissioned Marine Officers do not question the Orders signed by a Lieutenant Colonel." "I see, Major, and I quite agree with both what you did and why you did it. That is all - you are dismissed, Major".

The CG, 2nd MARDFV entered the room and addressed the Commandant. "Sir, I don't know any of the details, but your helo is standing by to take you to CPNC where your personal aircraft will take you to Andrews. There, you will be met by your Official car and taken to the White House for a meeting with the President- That is all I know at this time, Sir".

THE COMMANDANT MEETS WITH THE PRESIDENT

Right on schedule, the four-star General who is THE Commandant of the Marine Corps, found himself ushered into the Oval Office by the President's Chief of Staff. Notably absent were any Members of the Joint Chiefs of Staff of the Armed Forces. The President was standing behind his desk. He walked around the corner of the desk and motioned to the General to take a seat in an upholstered chair with arms in front of the desk. The President sat in another similar chair, facing him, a few feet away. The President began, "General, I would guess that you have no idea why you are here. Am I correct?" "Yessir, you are correct." "Well, you can relax, Marine. You are here so that I can get some facts about some recent incidents that are causing me some problems with some Representatives and at least one Senator. Frankly, Sir, I don't give a damned about a slew of Representatives whose Constituents have a personal problem with how or why you promote your Junior Officers. That's your business and you make those decisions in the way you see fit. You'll get no interference from me on any of those matters. I'm told you have a very young Major who should probably still be a First Lieutenant. Again, that is your business and none of mine. I begin to get a bit concerned when you ask the Navy's Senior JAG Officer to render a decision regarding a Contract with a Marine Officer who also has a Contract with the Central Intelligence Agency. You apparently wanted to know which Contract takes precedence. You apparently mentioned something about a Marine Officer's Contract being akin to "indentured servitude under the Constitution". "Is that correct or close to correct, Sir?" "Yes, Mr. President, it is. I admit to having used those words." "Poor choice of words, General. Essentially, that is true, but those particular words have an extremely negative connotation in the world of today. When people think of "indentured servitude", they don't think of a legal term -they think of black slavery in one particular era of our Nation's occasionally regrettable, inglorious past. The mischoice of words has been compounded by the fact that you apparently had a black Marine Master Sergeant working for the CIA in Iraq. That is just part of the bind you've put me in. Now, I've got the Director of the CIA defending his turf, saying that when his Agents want a Marine working for them, it is in the interests of National Security, which takes precedence over any "Contract" the Marine Corps may have with one of its Officers. To top it all, I've got the Chairman of the Senate Intelligence Committee, again, citing "National Security", insisting he can "tap" any damned body he wants to work for and report to him. Now, I can soothe any ruffled feathers with the CIA Director, but "pissing-off" the Chairman of the Senate Intelligence Committee is quite another matter. There are a number of pieces of pending legislation that I need passed by the Senate and, his Chairmanship of an important Committee aside, he is still a vote in the Senate, at a time when I dearly need 60 of them to cut-off debate to get the Bill I need passed and sent to the House Conference Committee, differences worked-out, and passed by the full House for me to sign into Law. Are you beginning to see the predicament you've placed me in, General? "I had no idea, Mr. President." "Of course you didn't. You're a trained, career Military Officer whose Marines are expected to fight and win battles in defense of their Country and the Constitution. You are not a Politician, although I will grant you that achieving the rank of four stars involves personalities, posturing, and, occasionally, pleasing when you probably would personally prefer not to have to do so. In the Corps, you achieve the Rank of Colonel by being damned good at your Military profession, demonstrating leadership on a daily basis, making the right decisions. Then, and only then, do you commit the troops under your Command, and accomplish your assigned Objectives with no or minimal loss of your Marines. When you are promoted to General, it's a whole new "ballgame". Leadership is left behind for the Colonels to supply. Your job becomes one of "how many troops are needed - how much equipment will be required, and what will be the actual cost versus budgeted funds available."

My job, as Commander-in-Chief, and the Congress'job in raising and allocating funds, is to either fully fund your needs, or restrict what you will be able to do by refusing to supply the funding to do so. That is my "take" on the situation you and I find ourselves in. Do you agree or do you have a rebuttal, General. If so, NOW is the time to express it. I hold no grudges. We both have our professional and personal opinions and I openly invite you to express yours, here and now. I doubt you'll have another occasion to meet, personally with me, here, informally, for the remainder of your term of Office as Commandant of the Marine Corps. Even if you are reluctant to say what is on your mind, HERE AND NOW is your only and last chance to say it, directly to the President with no others present. Either "spit it out" here and now, or take it to your grave, General. Anything you wish to say to me? No, Sir. Just tell me what you want me to do now to correct what you feel I may have done wrong. General, you will retain Marine Stabler as a Major. Have him report directly to the Commanding General, Fleet Marine Force-Atlantic, for further Orders, Directives, or Assignments. CGFMFLant will sign the Major's Officer Fitness Report and become his "report directly to" Authority. He will have no further contact with the Senator, nor will he have any further association with the CIA. I have directed that both of those relationships with Marine Stabler be terminated, retroactively to both my verbal and written instructions. Marines Westman and Stevens should be assured, by appropriate means, that their "TAD detour in Iraq" will have no adverse effect upon their careers. You will ensure that they are assigned, as appropriate, to a Unit within the Second Marine Division. Upon reporting to the CGFMFLant, Major Stabler will be assigned to attend your Force Recon School. Following that, he will be assigned to high-altitude survival School, and the Army's Paratrooper School at fort Benning, Georgia. I'm guessing that all of this will be accomplished by TAD Orders, during which time, he will be unavailable to CGFMFLant, but still reporting to that Command. It will be the Major's responsibility to ensure that that happens. I have been in contact with CGFMFLant, personally and he is not anxious to be assigned a Marine Officer with no training beyond TBS , but having worked for the CIA in Iraq. I'll mend my political fences with the good Senator. At such time as CGFMFLant no longer has the use or need for the Major' expertise or services, he will be released to HQMC for further assignment within the Marine Corps. You will be personally notified through your Chain of Command with myself and the Secretary of the Navy INFOED. General, as far as I am concerned, your career will not be adversely affected by either a most bizarre chain of events or this meeting with me. You are dismissed. Your Official car is waiting to take you back to your Office. Please give my best regards to your lovely wife, General. That is all.

RETURNING TO CONUS FOR
FURTHER DIRECTION

Major Martin Stabler caught a MARLOG (Marine Logistics - daily C-130 flight) out of Kuwait City to Marine Corps Air Station, Cherry Point, North Carolina. It would be a looong and boring flight at a cruising speed of about 600 miles an hour, with two "touchdowns for refueling" for the four-engine turbo-prop transport Aircraft. It was an amazing Aircraft, with its versatility and airworthiness. If need be, it could take-off (given enough runway) on three engines and remain aloft on two engines if they were not both on the same side of the fuscelage. It could take off from both an Aircraft Carrier and a SATS (Short Airfield for Tactical Support) facility using interlocking steel plates for runway surface instead of the customary concrete (the steel plates are known in Aviation circles as "Marsten Matting"). It could take-off using "JATO" (Jet-assisted take-off) bottles, bolted or clamped to the side of the fuscelage just behind the flight-deck - four on each side. When fired or "engaged/activated", by the pilot, they "kicked-in" during takeoff at about 85 to 100 MPH. They provided instant vertical lift up to about 100 feet. Then the plane would briefly seem to stall as the propellers of those four engines began to pull enough air over the top surface of the wings, to keep it airborne and begin forward flight.

Upon landing at Cherry Point, Marty caught a base taxi to the BOQ (Bachelor Officers' Quarters) in "Officers' Country", about a five mile drive down the main street of the base -Roosevelt Boulevard. There, he checked in, received his room key. his mattress cover (affectionately called a "fart sack"), bottom and top sheets, blanket, a handful of towels and the "duty bar" of Ivory soap. He went to his assigned room, undressed and went to bed, promptly falling asleep (nobody has yet to figure out how to sleep on a C-l 30 Hercules transport aircraft -the constant droning of the engines is a persistent low-pitch hum in your ears).

MCAS (Marine Corps Air Station), Cherry Point, NC is a sprawling facility directly on the Trent River, some 20 miles inland from the Atlantic. It is the Home of the Second Marine Aircraft Wing. The "Wing" (meaning just the aircraft and supporting equipment) is Commanded by a Major (two-star) General. The Base, itself (all of the buildings and related real estate) is Commanded by a Brigadier (one-star) General. The local town is Havelock, located halfway between New Bern and Morehead City/Atlantic Beach, North Carolina. About 50 miles to the Southeast, is Jacksonville, NC, Home of the Second Marine Division. About 50 miles inland, to the West is the "really sprawling" Seymour Johnson Air force Base" at Goldsboro, NC. Farther inland is the large US Army Base of "Fort Bragg" and its associated Airfield of Pope Air Base, which is largely used by helicopters. They are hosted by the City of Fayetteville, NC.

Marty was on "Tee-eh-Dee" (TAD for Temporary Additional Duty) Orders with no "Report by" date. That is extremely unusual and Marty knew he had to very careful when and if asked to show his Orders. He just had to avoid situations where that might occur. Any competent Administrative Officer would have known that something "really heavy" was going on and started asking questions that Major Stabler was not prepared to address. To make matters worse for Marty, First Lieutenants and Captains received TAD Orders, usually to attend a particular school. Majors didn't receive squat except a twice-monthly paycheck if they didn't screw up too bad., waiting to be selected for promotion to Lieutenant Colonel with its silver Oak Leaf rank insignia. "On the road" as he had been almost constantly, he had lost track of days of the week and the local time since he had been flipping through time zones like pages in a book. He went to the front desk and asked the Duty NCO what day it was - it was Sunday. Then, instinctively, he asked the time "Zulu" (a Marine Corps reference to 'local time" - Zulu was ALWAYS local time.) To get his room in the BOQ, he had shown his CIA ID Card to the Desk NCO, who didn't notice that the Issuer was the Central Intelligence Agency, only that the photo looked like him and the Rank was shown as Captain. That was good enough to get him a room. Now, he wanted to walk upstairs to the BOQ bar, known as The Dirty Shame, to have a few beers. The bar had picked up that name due to the fact that it was patronized almost exclusively by unmarried Officers who were dateless for the evening. Therefore, they had no choice but to drink there where it was a "Dirty Shame" that they were forced to drink either alone, or among other Officers who found themselves in the same situation. A small but "dedicated" group of mostly young Officers were entertaining themselves by playing various bar games using dice. There was "Ship-Captain - Crew" and "twenty-one-Aces-for-the-bar". Even at the low price of drinks on a Military Base, you didn't want to get in on "twenty-one-Aces…." unless you were sure that all players were drinking just beer. Just a couple of Martini drinkers could cost you plenty if you threw the "twenty-first-Ace". If a dozen or more were playing, a loss could cost you thirty or forty bucks in less than twenty minutes. Inebriation was not a particular concern, since almost everyone just had to navigate down just one floor and a couple of doors and they could "crash into bed". Looked at another way, it was relatively cheap entertainment that didn't require driving off the Reservation and risking a drunk-driving ticket by either the local Police or the Base Military Police.

Monday morning came and Marty called a Base taxi to take him to the Provost Marshall's Office to get a new Marine Corps Military ID Card with his photo and showing his Rank as Major. He did that. - whew, that was over and done with. There had been no questions asked and no proof requested of him, other than to show and surrender his old ID which showed him as a First Lieutenant. The Sergeant processing his new ID card, as it happened, was just doing his job without paying any particular attention to any of the details. He didn't give a "fat,happy, rat's ass how you went from First Lieutenant to Major without surrendering a Card showing you as a Captain. It was like, "hey, Sir, you give me one valid ID Card and I'll give you a replacement, as long as I get one from you, you'll get a newer one from me. That's all I care about". Marty was most grateful for the absence of either interrogation or prying questions. He left the Office of the PMO with a current head-shot photo (with non-regulation longish hair) and the Rank of Major-That's all he cared about, right now - that was all that mattered for the moment. He was finished with his work here at Cherry Point. Now he was headed to Washington and would arrange to fly into Boiling Air force Base in northern Virginia. Marty caught a "hop" on an unscheduled C-l17 aircraft (it just landed, discharged someone and spun around for immediate take-off when Marty ran out onto the tarmac waving his arms and hands. The Crewchief saw him and opened the rear door and dropped the staircase. Marty ran up the stairs. The crewchief removed one ear of his headset and Marty said something to him. The Crewchief assisted Marty aboard, pulled up the folding staircase, closed the door and secured it. Marty took a seat and secured his seatbelt. The two propeller-driven engines roared to life and in less than a minute, they were "wheels-up" and on their way to Boiling, just outside of Washington.

It was a short flight to Boiling and they landed as scheduled. Marty went to the Officers' Club and had a beer. He then caught a ride to the Main Gate at the Annex for Anacostia Naval Air Station, just across the Potomic river from the Capitol. He asked for and got a ride in an MP Jeep to the Officers' Club which was very small and quaint.. The bar was on the second deck (floor) and had maybe a dozen barstools in addition to maybe a dozen tables. It was a nice, secluded, quiet place where Marine helo pilots, flying the Government area, came to relax after a day of doing "touch-and-goes" at various rooftop helipads in the area, particularly Walter Reed Army hospital. They were backed-up by "Marine One" helos flying, daily, training/fam (familiarization) flights out of the small helicopter Base at Quantico, Virginia. It was here, of all places, where Marty found himself in a most uncomfortable situation.

Now that he had a current Marine Military ID Card, he was wearing a new set of Marine "Greens" and wearing his Major's Gold Oak leaves on both his shoulders and shirt collars. From the dimly-lit far side of the bar he heard a voice. "Don't I know you, Marine?" "I don't have a clue" came the answer from Marty - "who'se asking", was the best Marty could do on short notice, having been taken totally by surprise. "You're Stabler, aren't you, from OCS and TBS.1' Marty shot back, "Well who hi the hell wants to know - Step over in the light where I can see you and make yourself known - I'll buy you a beer - is that a deal or what?" The answer came, "Well, shit, yeah. Your old Classmate, Jim Anderson, here - bull (very senior - lots of time in Grade) First Lieutenant, here. Should make the promotion list for Captain - the (Selection) Board just met. What the hell are you doing wearing Major's leaves - who the fuck do you know that me and the rest of our Class don't?" "Goddam, what the hell do I say now to THE MOUTH, Jim Anderson?" If I say the wrong thing, 300 Marine First Lieutenants will be calling CMC (Commandant of the Marine Corps) tomorrow wanting to know how I got to be a fucking Major so fast. Somebody will know a newspaper Reporter or Congressman and be asking questions and demanding answers. I don't need this shit and neither does my boss, the Senator. There's no telling where it will lead or end.

Marty would soon find out. The next morning, he got a knock on his door in the Anacostia BOQ. It was a Marine Pfc telling Major Stabler that he had a personal call at the front desk. White boxer shorts flapping in the breeze and white tee shirt, Marty answered the phone. It was a Colonel at HQMC (Headquarters, Marine Corps) wanting to know what Major Stabler was doing at Anacostia Naval Air Station on Open-ended PCS Orders issued by the CIA. "Major, are you under the impression that either Saddam or Al-Qaeda are lurking somewhere at Anacostia?" "No, sir. I am in-transit and this is just a stop along the way to use Government air for travel." "Very well, Major. For some strange reason I accept your explanation. Now get the hell out of there and get about going wherever the hell it is you are going. Some buddy of yours from Basic School is raising hell with CMC about how come you're a Major and he and your Classmates are still hoping to get promoted to Captain. I'll handle it from this end, but I need you to get gone and fast. Langley is looking for you, too, and some Senator's Chief-of-Staff wants you to contact him ASAP. Now, move out, Major - MOVE -MOVE-MOVE. That is all - out!

Marty decided he had to get back into civilian clothes. His Marine Uniform with its Gold Leaves was raising too many questions and he could not afford another encounter with a buddy he had known at The Basic School. He took a taxi to CIA Headquarters at Langley, out in the Virginia countryside, adjacent to John Foster Dulles International Airport, showed his wallet ID Card and asked to see the person in Charge of Senate Liaison. He was shown to a small Conference Room while waiting for Whomever. Shortly, a middle-aged man entered the room, stuck out his right hand and blurted out "Semper Fi, Marty. I'm the Senator's Senior Military Aide. All you need to know about me is that I am a Marine Lieutenant Colonel. I'll be conducting all meetings with you here. I'm CLEARED to hear anything you might have to say to the Senator, and Goddammit, try not to run into anyone else in the Corps who was part of your Basic Class. You've got a shitload of First Lieutenants asking about promotions. It's just a matter of time before a boatload of Captains will want to know why we "went below the Zone" and how far below it we went, to pick you up for Major. They'll be wondering if they've now had their first, unofficial passover for promotion. I doubt you remember, but back in 1968 a gob of Captains got fucked-over really bad for promotion when President Lyndon Johnson ordered CMC to go far below the Zone to pick up his son-in-law, Captain Chuck Robb for promotion to Major. In doing so, it had the practical effect of raising a red flag for all those between Robb and the Selection Zone, when the met the next time around. The Board became preoccupied in looking for "problems that did not exist" with each of those unfortunate Captains. Not knowing the circumstances, details, and lacking any other information, the Board set its own criteria for Selection to Major. That criteria became the awarding of either a Bronze or Silver Star (or higher personal decoration). A lot of good and deserving Captains got screwed over in that fiasco. We do not need a repeat of that situation resulting from your promotion. AND, oh yes, the Senator wants you "fast-tracked" to Lieutenant Colonel since you'll need at least that much Rank to go where we're going to send you next. For these reasons, and the reasons I believe you have most recently discovered, the Senator doesn't want you anywhere NEAR his Senate Office, or the Capitol, either, for that matter. Now what's all this about the Moussad Agent being in Mosul. What can you tell me about him and what he was doing in Kurdish territory? The Senator is most interested in the details of that situation. Marty briefed the Colonel and was given Orders to return to Mosul to gather a lot more information and DETAILS.

MAJOR STABLER'S PROBLEM

Marty was no in a state of "Limbo", and he knew it. First, he had to report in to the Chief of Staff of the Commanding General, Fleet Marine Force - Atlantic. That person was a Navy Captain (a four-striper, in Service lingo). It went like, "Sooo, you're the infamous Marine Major who is almost literally on Permanent T-A-D Orders. I feel for you, Mr. Stabler. You're a Marine who has never had PCS Orders (Permanent Change of Station). You're a Jarhead, a Grunt, who has never served in one particular Unit, much less Commanded one. Some Senator snatched your ass out of Basic School, which you never got to complete, assigned you to the CIA for Overseas "snooping and pooping". You were looking for shit that probably didn't exist and never did exist. If you were to find it, you would embarrass the hell out of Mr. Hans Blix and the entire United Nations WMD Inspection Team. Sooo, again, you were 'expected' to turn up nothing new. Yet you were working for a Democrat Senator with considerable 'clout', trying to catch a Republican President lying to the Country about Saddam's WMDs as an excuse for Invading Iraq? Does that about sum it all up, Mr. Stabler?" "You are amazingly well informed, Captain?" "Not really, Major. Your story is "scuttlebutt" (rumors) all over the Navy. Actually, you're a celebrity, of sorts. Everybody thinks you're either some kind of a 'mystery man' and want no part of you, or you just got your ass in one incredible sling and are just trying to get your Marine Corps career back on track. They'll work with you just for curiosity. My advice to you is to get these three training assignments completed so that you're at least somewhat qualified to be Major and of use to some Command. As it is now, we have to accept you because of what the President ordered the Commandant to do. We do not need your services now and we have nothing for you to do until you get a shitload of further training. I've arranged for you to attend Recon School, Jump School, and High Altitude Training School. You'll do

Recon at LeJeune, Jump at Fort Benning, and High Altitude at Pickle Meadows out of Pendleton. That should take you a good six months. THEN report back here, to me for further assignment. Right now, I thinking of an assignment at NOB (Naval Operations Base) Norfolk, Breezy Point Naval Air Station, or Little Creek Amphibious Operations Base. If timing is good, you might just squeeze in Amphibious Warfare School at Quantico. You can probably forget about spending any time with a Marine Infantry Unit for the duration of your Career. I've just got to get you a crapload of formal training you should have had before you were promoted to Major. I'll see you back here in six to eight months. At that time, we'll see how best you can be of service to the Missions we have in this Command. You'll start at LeJeune for Force Recon and if you're not in decent shape, they'll run your ass ragged. Then on to Army Jump School at Benning in Georgia, then on to Pickle Meadows where you'll freeze what's left of you ass off. A couple of words of caution. You're still young and single. Don't get drunk and get your ass tossed in the brig by the MPs. You're free to 'pork' any broad you wish, but don't get any of them pregnant or you'll be dead-meat to both the Corps and the Navy. There's not much of a market in the civilian world , either, for warmed-over Marine Majors with a history of unintentional fuck-ups. If you should happen to date a lass whose father turns out to be a United States Senator, kiss.her both goodnight and goodbye. That is all, Major Stabler. Now get your ass out of here before the CG happens to walk in and see you and you put my ass in a bigger wringer than yours is already in. That is all - get gone !" "Aye-aye, Sir." That's just great, Marty mused to himself. Here I am, a Marine Major who should be just a senior First Lieutenant and nobody wants me because I happened to meet one United States Senator too many and got my ass shanghaied onto Permanent TAD OUTSIDE OF THE MARINE CORPS. The Commandant himself bitched about it to the Navy Judge Advocate General which got the Commandant involved, trying to help me. The President called the Commandant "on the carpet" trying to find out exactly what's going on, how it all happened and why it happened at all. The Commandant was "blindsided" by it all and had nothing to tell the President. That did not sit well with the Commander-in-Chief, who had both cheeks of the Commandant's ass for lunch. Marty got "shoveled-off' to the

CGFMFLant who neither wanted Marty nor needed him. Sooo, now he's going to a lot of Schools, trying to play "catch-up" ball, and he had no idea where he's going to end up, EXCEPT that he will not be Commanding a Marine Infantry Unit. In all likelihood, he never will be. That virtually eliminates any chance at a Bronze or Silver Star to get him to either Lieutenant Colonel, or Colonel. Shit, why me?

He wasn't due to report in to Force Recon School at LeJeune for nearly three weeks. No point in getting there early, since the last thing he needs is to be on TAD Orders on a Marine Infantry Base and not assigned to any particular Command Every Battalion's Administrative Officer would open his OQR (Officer's Qualification Record) and see how he got to be Major.It would be assumed that he was a "flunkie" who knew a lot of people in very high places and kissed their asses BIG TIME, for rapid promotion. Nothing he could say or do would erase the suspicion. He hadn't even been at TBS long enough to get to the Rifle Range and qualify on both the rifle and pistol. Therefore, he had no "badges" to wear over his left breast pocket. His only Ribbon was the National Defense Service. If it were not for the Gold leaves on his collar, he might be mistaken for a Marine Private. Bummer !

He drove to Quantico and checked into "Casual Company" close to Mainside, with his TAD Orders. They had nothing available for him to do, so he got a lift to the Quantico helicopter field, Home of Marine One and the rest of the Presidential Helicopter Squadron. There, for several weeks, he took "sightseeing hops", while the Pilots and Crew did recon "dry-runs" over the entire Capital Area. They also did "touch-and-go's" onto the rooftop helipads for Walter Reed Army Hospital, the Senate, the US House, the East lawn of the White House, and various other sites where they might be called upon to land.

Finally, it came time to report for Recon School. It was rough, but he made it through. Then, on to Army Fort Benning, Georgia, for Jump (Paratrooper) School, which was a breeze. He used a "static line" (your rip-cord is snapped onto a steel clothes line inside the Cargo plane). When you jump through the plane's open door, your rip cord quickly gets taught and jerks open your small "primary" chute. When you are well clear of the aircraft, the inflated small chute jerks open your main parachute. They were not permitted to manually pull their own "D" rings until their last jump, and even then, it was voluntary. The reason given is that it was a "safety" issue, to almost eliminate mistakes and errors. To anyone's memory, no Main chute had ever failed to open and fully deploy when a static line jump was used. Marty finished Jump School. FINALLY, he had a badge to wear over his left-breast pocket - Jump Wings. NOW, I'm finally getting somewhere, he thought to himself. Maybe that Navy Captain had a good plan to save his career, after all. Then it was time to report in to Camp Pendleton for High Altitude Training. He, and about a dozen others, were transported by a standard USMC."Six-by", heavy-duty truck, to a location well above the "snow/frost" line in the Sierra Nevada Mountains. They passed a crude, wooden sign painted in traditional Marine manner - red background with yellow lettering - "USMC Training Facility - Welcome to Pickle Meadows". They drove to a row of steel Quonset Huts. A Marine Captain came out to greet them. He said, "Welcome to Marine Corps Paradise, gentlemen. For the next two weeks, you will enjoy my hospitality. You will listen to my Instructors and take heed, or you will literally freeze to death - the choice is entirely yours. We have plastic body-bags awaiting any of you who may decide that you already know how to live up here and we're all full of crap. Up here, it's colder than the average morgue, so we can just leave your corpse outside until the Class finishes and the same truck that brought you comes to take you back. No nasty rotting body - you are literally frozen stiff. Hell, some of you may feel that way, anyway, and just not realize that you are still alive with just a slight problem with moving your joints and limbs. Can we Medevac you out of here, if needed? Yes, we can, but not by helo. See those two metal poles over there? We string a steel cable between them. We hook to that cable a steel line attached to the back of a special harness we strap to you. A C-130 flies low over our site dragging a kind of tail hook from its lowered rear ramp. The tail hook snags the cable stretched between those two poles and takes it and you airborne. A winch in the back of the C-130 pulls you up and into the cargo hold and delivers you to nearby El Toro Marine Air Base, where an ambulance is waiting. So far, we've never had to perform that exercise. While here, you will eat nothing but MREs. You will hike, daily, at least five miles in knee-to-thigh-deep snow. Nothing is "simulated" here, gentlemen. Trust me, it is all for real and you will learn to adapt to it successfully or you will suffer the consequences - failure to complete your assigned Mission - possible loss of life - your troops or yours. For safety reasons, we do have one snow mobile and one Sno-Cat tracked vehicle. I am the only person with authority to dispatch either vehicle and I have never found it necessary to do so. Your instructors will decide when and if it is necessary to change your boots to use wooden show shoes. In that case, you will tie your bootlaces together and wear your boots around your neck. You will put on deerskin Indian mukluks that lace with rawhide to your knees. This will allow the balls of your feet and toes to move downward through a slot in the snowshoe to provide you with traction over the snow. This will allow you to "slide and glide" over the top of the snow. If you should decide to stop and regroup while on showshoes, be very careful to just squat on your snowshoes. Do not attempt to step off the showshoes, since you are probably atop up to ten feet of snow. If that should happen, when you stop falling, curl up in a ball, breathe shallowly to conserve your energy, and wait for help. An Instructor will call in a CH-53 helicopter that will drop you a harness to put on and then extract you by winch-cable. AND, you will have failed the Course for failure to listen to your instructors. One last thought- There are some Native Indians in this area who use these mountains for their tribal burials. They use "funeral pyres" in their ritual. The deceased is laid atop a wooden structure set above ground on wooden poles about ten feet high. This is an offering and appeasement to their "Great God of the Sky and Heavens" - their "Jesus, Allah, Mohammed, Buddha, whatever". After a mourning period of a duration determined by that tribe's Chief, a pile of wood and brush, underneath the elevated body is set afire, as their form of cremation. If your patrol should come across a pyre still in mourning, but before it has been burned, you may stop and "pay your respects to the deceased", but do not get off your snowshoes. The body is just above the snow which is probably five to ten feet deep. One of my Instructors did that once, but managed to grab on to the log platform holding the body of the deceased. A couple of "Students" managed to pull him back on top of the snow long enough for him to put his snowshoes back on and stand up. There is no written Exam for this Course. The "final exam", as it were, will be most interesting, I promise you. It will be "individualized/personalized" - kind of like playing a round of golf. You'll be entirely by yourself in terms of execution of the exercise, sooo, if you come up short, you'll have nobody to blame but yourself. You'll have no "bragging rights" back at your Unit. That is all, gentlemen. I'll see you back here in two weeks when you board the truck for your return to the Main Base -no Certificates or Plaques to hang on your wall. Just your personal memories of your visit to "Paradise at Pickle Meadows". Good luck to you all.

Marty finished the course without "incident" and a handshake from the Good Captain told him that he has "passed" his two weeks in "Paradise at Pickle Meadows". Now to report back to the Navy Captain at HQ,CGFMFLant, Norfolk, Virginia. He did so and there was still nothing for him to do there. He returned to Quantico and reported in, again, to Casual Company. He was told that at the FBI Agent Training School, just behind the Base Headquarters Building, there was a Class in session. He might want to check it out. With time on his hands, still on Permanent TAD Orders, three formal Schools to his credit, and no pending assignment at FMFLant, what the hell? He'd go and check it out. It would prove to be the best decision he had ever made in his entire life, both now and for his next "career". He was able to "audit" several Classes, sitting in a chair at the back of the room. One Class was taught by a Special Agent Robert Carlos Ruiz. During a break, Agent Ruiz came up to him, saw his Major's leaves and his Jump Wings and asked, "Major, to what do I owe the pleasure of you auditing ray class?". Marty said, "just idle curiousity, Sir. The Marine Corps has me on Permanent TAD Orders - it's a long story, Sir. Fm between assignments which may or may not come to reality. I heard you were teaching some classes, here at the Academy, and I thought Id' pass some time and listen in". Agent Ruiz shook Marty's hand and then put his left arm around Marty's shoulder, saying, "I have something that may interest you, Major, stick around and see me here, after the Class, okay?" "You bet, Sir."

Special Agent Ruiz' topic was "under what conditions can you chase a suspected kidnapper or Bank robber, with hostages, across State lines and place him or her under arrest? Since almost all FBI Agents have a Degree in Law, the question was to test their knowledge of the Federal Mann Act. Certain "elements" had to exist in order for such a pursuit to be legal and stand up in Federal Court. Would a Federal Grand

Jury have to be convened to determine if "evidence" supported the actual existence of those "elements". Would the "witness" of another Agent involved in the actual chase be sufficient, legal "corroboration", or would that be "considered self-serving, defensive evidence" and, therefore, tainted?" Wow, thought Marty, to himself - this is some deep shit and very interesting. After his lecture, Special Agent Ruiz met Marty at the rear of the room and invited him to a cup of coffee at a nearby vendor.

"Major, I know very little about your situation, but what little I do know is that you're a bit of a "man without a Country", as it were. A Marine without either a Mission or a Unit. Am I at all close to target?" "Sir, you're not only close - you're dead on target." "Well, I may be able to help you over the long term. Would you be interested in what I have to offer, considering that to accept it, you have to give up both your Rank and your Marine Corps career very shortly and accept a GS Rating with the Federal Government with a guaranteed Federal Retirement?" "This is very heady stuff, Mr. Ruiz. Specifically, what are you talking about? I can't deal in broad generalities and give you a decision. Can you lay it out for me in some detail and, more importantly, for me, is, do you have the Authority to offer to me whatever it is you're going to, perhaps, offer me?" "Major, the answer is, definitely, yes, I do have the authority. We both know that talk is cheap and bullshit is deep." They were sitting at a small round coffee table. Ruiz motioned Stabler to come closer. Ruiz placed his forearms and hands flat on the table and wiggled his index finger for Stabler to do so also. With their heads no more than a foot apart, Ruiz whispered, "I'm Secret Service and assigned to the Presidential Detail. I am personally responsible for the President's safety when he travels. I have no involvement when the President is in the District. I have a female Assistant who I have reasons to believe is wrestling with some personal problems, the nature of which is none of my concern. I do not wish to go into any further detail on that situation and you do not have a "need to know". I will shortly find a reason to hire a replacement Agent. You've been to Recon School, Jump School, and Pickle Meadows. Those three schools are prime criteria to fill the job I'm going to need filled. Are you interested? Do you want the job? No hedging your bets, Major. I know your situation. Right here and now, Sir, do you want the job - yes or no -I need to know right here and now, Sir?" Marty felt a huge lump in his throat and he was somewhat "swimmy-headed" - God help me - what do I do? Talk to me God ! Then there was a seemingly interminable silence as the two men's eyes met in a cold stare across the table - maybe a foot from one another. Marty took a very deep breath, inhaled, and slowly exhaled, gained his composure, and softly replied, "yes, Mr. Ruiz, I want the job." "Great, Major Stabler. Give me a number where you can be reached. Either me or my people will be in touch with you shortly for paperwork to join you to the FBI and separate you from the Marine Corps. No more Permanent TAD Orders for you, Major. Welcome aboard, MARTY. Oh yes, Marty - there is one thing I cannot do for you and I suggest you do it tomorrow. You need to write a letter to the Commandant of the Marine Corps, resigning your Commission, effective immediately. Even though you are a Major, you may not have fulfilled your three-year initial commitment following your finishing OCS. However, given your past and the problems you have inadvertantly caused the Commandant, I see no reason for the Corps to refuse to release you from your initial contractual agreement. If there is some snag, I'll have the Director of the FBI work it out with the Marine Command so that you can start training with me and my Team immediately. I'll see you right back here in a week with your new FBI Credentials. Till then, stay loose, cool, and out of trouble, please.

All of the necessary Orders and other paperwork went without a hitch. His intention and his dream of Commanding Marines in a Platoon, Company, Battalion, or Regiment, were now gone with the stroke of a pen on a piece of paper. He would never be a Colonel of Marines and would never lead any Marine in combat. Perhaps, he never WOULD HAVE, who would know? He reminded himself of the C&W song by Kenny Rogers - "The Gambler" - and the lines, "you've go to know when to hold and know when to fold". Marty had HELD as long as he could. The time had come to FOLD.

He reported in to Special Agent Ruiz, at the FBI Academy at Quantico. It felt really weird to pass through the Main Gate at Quantico without flashing a Marine Corps ID Card and getting saluted by the Guard. Instead, he had to ask the Gate guard to phone the FBI Academy and get "authenticated" to Pass the Gate and enter the Base. He was now a GS-16 Rating and an FBI Field Agent in a business suit.

He learned that, like the Navy, all personnel of "Officer" rank, went by "Mr." and their last name. Ruiz gave him the Standard-Issue, Glock 9 mm semiautomatic pistol. AH of the "rounds" had special loads of powder and primer, since they would potentially be fired aboard Air Force One in flight. Each bullet had lethal power up to aboutlO or 12 feet-only to minimize the possibility of penetrating the skin of the Aircraft and causing catastrophic, rapid decompression. The choice of a shoulder holster or a belt paddle holster was his. He was given a specially formatted "short Course" for the Law he would need to know and "hands-on" training in how to apply handcuffs in crowded spaces and places, without attracting "undue attention". He would do this constantly, even in Class with other Agents, male and female. He learned how to either avoid or "parry" a knee to the groin. How to deal with those skilled in the Martial Arts. How to deal with those either grossly overweight or drunk or both. The most difficult situation was having to either seal-off or clear out a Pool Hall along the route of a Presidential Motorcade. On the Presidential Detail, Agents didn't talk "into their sleeves" -that was all "Hollywood crap". They didn't wear "earpieces", either. They had a micro-chip radio with a micro-transmitter and pea-sized battery surgically-implanted just under the skin on the topside of the right clavicle (collarbone). It required a quarter-inch incision. It was always in transmit-only mode, since on the "PD", information and orders were given with no need to receive. The micro-transmitter had a range of, maybe, three miles, and was largely line-of-sight. The tiny battery was good for about a year.. The only "bugaboo", was that the device was constantly "live" and incredibly sensitive (you did not have to talk toward your right shoulder), so you had to remember to "deactivate" it by simply speaking your personal code. It would automatically reactivate after 8 hours (preprogrammed to allow for 8 hours of sleep), unless it received the Code earlier.

The next day, Special Agent Ruiz met with Special Agent Carla Marie Edwards. He told her that he was removing her from the Airborne Presidential Detail, since it was his feeling that she needed some tune to attend to her own family life. It would not be a negative reflection on her performance of her duties, but his personal decision on who could best perform the most demanding job in the Federal Government, outside of the Presidency, itself. He told her that he expected her to receive his decision as the "professional" Agent that she was, without question, and without request for review, Administrative OR Judicial. She had been trained to accept such decisions and he expected her to remember her training and act accordingly. Agent Ruiz added, "Agent Edwards, er, Marie, personally, I believe you're entitled to know a bit more than I am authorized to tell you. Besides, you'll still be with the 'Service', assuming you wish to continue, and we are a relatively small group and 'word' travels fast. My new Assistant will be a Marine Corps Major who has decided to leave the Corps for personal reasons, in order to join the PD. He has been trained in reconnaissance, is a paratrooper and a high-altitude Operations Specialist. Those are all skills I believe I'm going to be needing with what I have been told is the recovery and the resurgence of the Al Qaida following the Events of 9-11, the War in Iraq, and the War in Afghanistan. Marie, I wish you well. You've done a fine job for me. I think you're better suited for the PD when the President is either "in the District" or "on the ground" in CONUS. I'll give you a fine recommendation for further Assignment. That is all - you are dismissed".

Okay, Agent Marty Stabler, here's the Big Bird - Air Force One. She's one big Mutha and loaded-for-bear. This IS the flying White House. It can do everything for the President that the actual White House can do. And I DO mean EVERY GODDAMNED THING. Now its easy to ger preoccupied with this huge symbol of American Democracy and the airborne Home of the Leader of the Free World. BUT, your job has absolutely nothing to do with this huge airplane, UNLESS, the President, or the first lady, or their children happen to be aboard. Then, and only then, does it become your concern. The Goddamned jet can be blown to a million pieces in flight and it is of no particular concern to you (other than as a taxpayer who helped pay for it), IF the President was not aboard at the time. Your job is to protect the President. The Vice President, SECDEF, SECSTATE, WHOEVER, might be blown to bits - it isn't your problem. Your concern and your ONLY concern is the President and his immediate family. Now go to Walter Reed and get yourself surgically implanted. Then report to the White House Chief-of-Staff and await further instructions from me. Now, get outta here.

The next morning, Marty was having coffee in the Officers' Closed Mess (COM-C) at Anacostia Naval Air Station when he got a call from

Agent Ruiz. "Agent Stabler, you will go to the Control Tower and ask the Officer-on-Duty to contact Marine- One-Alpha on "button Blue", with instructions to touch down at NAS Anacostia to pick up one male passenger in civilian clothing and transport him directly to Andrews for a briefing. You will be that passenger. I will meet you there. That is all - Ruiz, out. Marty did as instructed. Marine One Alpha landed adjacent to the Control Tower at AFB Andrews. Ruiz quickly greeted him. "Stabler, I hope you've got one hell of a good memory, 'cause I don't have the time to go over all that we've talked about and touched on. It's "performance time" and you're about to be 'in the thick of it', as it were. Ready or not, it's 'launch time'. Stay in my shadow and I'll make the introductions, as necessary."

"Good Morning, Captain Johnson, Sir. This is my new Assistant, Special Agent Stabler -Marty Stabler. My former Assistant, Marie, had to be reassigned to "District" for personal family concerns. Agent Stabler is a former Marine Major. He has been very well schooled and trained. If the need should arise, he can jump from your Big Bird at up to "Angels" 35 without oxygen and with you strapped to his back. He can fight-off all sorts of nasty critters, while keeping you safe, and do it all at 35,000 feet above mean sea level. Just imagine what he can do in protecting the President?" "Nice to meet you, Agent Stabler, and welcome aboard. I sincerely hope that neither the crew nor I will ever have need for your services. My job is to fly my passengers safely from wheels-up to touch down and taxi to a stop. If, among my passengers, is the President of the United States, so be it. I'm an Air Force Officer, a Citizen, a Patriot, a taxpayer. I do my job to the best of my ability. Been doing it for over 25 years, now. So far, no complaints or accidents. Welcome aboard, Agent Stabler, was it? Enjoy the ride. The President, Paul Cameron, is an easy-going decent sort. I just shake his hand and get Mm to where he wants to go."

Marty, this is the Crew Chief of Air force One. He'll give you a full brief of the security aboard the Aircraft. This is very different from the Hollywood movie "Air force One", where Actor Harrison Ford played the President and Actress Glen Close played the Vice President. If something should go wrong once we're airborne, the President doesn't go rummaging through luggage in the cargo hold looking for a cell phone. There are no weapons stored in any cabinets on the aircraft, period. All weapons are concealed on the bodies of the Federal Agents on board. It is not possible for an Agent to call in sick and be replaced. If an Agent fails to show for a flight, we fly with one less Agent. If there should be some kind of an epidemic, Air force Two is always standing by with a full crew. We simply transport the President and Captain Johnson to the other Aircraft which is identical to this one. The only delay would be caused by Captain Johnson having to take the time to go through his pre-flight procedures with another Co-pilot, Navigator, and Flight Engineer. That's a delay of fifteen minutes, max. The second bird is already fully-fueled and ready to go. Any questions? No, that about covers everything I can think of. Okay, we've got a flight planned to Denver and the President is due to come aboard shortly. Here he comes now - right on schedule. Marty, get to the back of the plane and check out your implant radio. Remember, it is not a normal "radio check" - you'll get no response. I'll come back to you and let you know if your equipment is working properly - your gear is "transmit-only". I'll tell our guys hi Denver when we're "wheels-up". When I walk by and tap you on the shoulder, you can kick back and snooze. When you feel your ears pop, we'll be on final approach into Denver at 5000 feet above Sea Level and time to go to work again. Job's 90% pleasure and 10% pure hell or anticipation of same. Life's a bitch, ain't it - yeah ! None of us in it for the money - that's for DAMNED sure. I've always figured it's part pure Patriotism and part knowing that you're the best of the elite. When we're up there (Ruiz pointed his right index finger straight up over his right shoulder), we're in-charge. We may take suggestions from the Pilot or the President, but the final decision is ours to make and we cannot be overruled, period. We may get out ass royally kicked when the Big Bird lands, but until then, it's all OUR CALL to make. Sometimes I think of myself as the homeplate Umpire in the 7th game of the World Series. Bottom of the ninth inning, score tied, bases loaded, two outs. The count is 3 and 2 on a contact-hitter. The pitch is a nasty curve ball - comes to the plate fat as a watermelon, right down the middle. Then it breaks sharply down-and-outside. Catcher has to lunge to get it. Runner from third starts to trot home with the winning run. The batter holds back and takes the pitch. Do I end the World Series on a ball-four walk ? Do rule it crossed the plate in the strike zone, the batter is out and send the game into extra innings? No question in my mind about it. It's where the pitch crossed the plate that matters. The batter was "fishing for a walk" to end the game the easy way - ball four and walk-in the winning run. Not on my watch, that doesn't happen. The batter could just as easily have reached a bit outside and "nine-ironed" that ball just over second base to drive-in the winning run. I'm not about to end a 165-game Season with a walked-in run unless the pitcher actually did throw ball-four. Yes, I am a Baseball fan. And, no, when Big Bird is in Denver, I'm too damned busy to take in a Rockies Game at Coors Field. Besides, what's a game without a few beers and that's a no-no while you're working. Okay, enough about that -it's time to go to work - no rest for either the professionals or the insane - pick your personal poison, Stabler. Main door's open, crew is lining up and locking the stairs hard against Big Bird. Local FBI and Police are in place. Air Force C-130 had unloaded the President's limo, AND -guess what? It's Show Time for President Cameron, It's time for the Locals to "shine in the limelight and justify their overtime pay. We'll only get involved if something goes very wrong or not according to plan or if there is a schedule change. Remember, always remember, our "comm" is only one-way and relatively short range. Our people were involved with the Advanced Team. We're "Federal" and the Law strictly defines the limits of our role and power when we're actually on-the-ground in any given State. Now, let's get back to Big Bird and see if Captain Johnson' flight schedule has been updated, altered, or changed. If it has, we don't want to be the last to know.

See, didn't I tell 'ya? There's been a change of plans. The White House wants the President to go to Chicago next to talk to the Union Brass for the UAW. There's talk of a possible strike by the Machinists and sympathy strikes by the AFL-CIO. The President needs to meet with their Board of Governors to try to avoid a strike. In Chicago, we're always "cleared" into O'Hare, since it's closest to Downtown, where almost all meetings take place. He's also been asked to visit a Public School for the Gifted and Talented in Science and Math who are looking into possible Federal Assistance to buy new laptop computers. NOW, we both know where we're going next. How about that shit, huh? We've got some rare "down time", so enjoy.

OH NO; NOT AGAIN, COULD IT BE?

President Cameron had ended his visit to Chicago's School for the Gifted and Talented. He was on the phone to his Secretary of Education. He had returned to Air Force One and it was about 4:30 PM Local Central Time. That made it 5:30 PM Eastern Time - an hour later. He wanted the Secretary to contact Dell, Hewlett-Packard, IBM, Compaq, Sony, Toshiba, and any other computer companies to see about a donation of advanced laptops to the Chicago School. Agent Ruiz gave the President the "time out" sign with his two hands. The President put his hand over the telephone receiver to hear Agent Ruiz say, "Sir, something has happened which needs your immediate attention". "What is it, Ruiz?" "Mr. President, I've just received confirmed information that the PanAm Building has "imploded", as in, come crashing down on top of Grand Central Station at 42 Street in New York City". "What - what say you ?" "Sir, there are no details yet,. Apparently there is no peripheral damage to any other buildings. It's almost as if a professional demolition Company had been hired to bring down the building directly to the ground with no adjacent damage. I can tell you that it happened at the busiest time for evening rush hour with thousands of commuters returning to the suburbs on Long Island to the East, and Westchester County and Connecticut to the North. New Jersey commuters are not immediately affected since their trains go out of Penn Station. The railroads involved are the Long Island Lines and the New York,New Haven, and Hartford Lines. All tram cars lined up to leave the Terminal had to have been crushed under the weight of the falling debris - reinforced concrete pillars and structural steel What authorities know so far is that no explosions were heard and the only form of fuel detectable came from ruptured utility pipes. Thankfully, there have been no secondary explosions detected so far. That is all I know at this time, Sir." "I guess you know the next question I'm about to ask, don't you?" "Sir, I would guess the possibility or probability of any terrorist involvement." "Bingo, how'd you guess ?" "Sir, I'd also be asking if there were any of the footprints or earmarks of an Al Qaeda involvement ? My guess would be that those would turn-up fairly quickly if they existed. From what little I know and from what I have been able to glean, Al Qaeda has become much more sophistocated since using airplanes as manned guided missiles. It's not that there is any shortage of martyrs for their cause of Islamic world domination and Fundamentalism, but morale is much higher when you can achieve your goals without the loss of any Operatives. WE do it by using unmanned drones instead of risking the lives of highly-trained pilots. There is something to be said for using your head instead of your hands and feet. How do you "implode" a building, anyway ? You damage its structural underpinnings and supports. In the case of the Pan Am Building, it was erected above the existing Grand Central Station by sinking reinforced concrete pillars twenty feet into the bedrock of Manhattan below all of the tracks for the trains. The building itself was constructed in the mid-to-late 1960s, so the concrete in those pillars has long-since fully cured out. I doubt the rebar has rusted at all or otherwise been strength-compromised. Just what other possibilities are left - not many ? I'd be looking at some form of acid (maybe Muriatic), that could eat into and corrode concrete. The plastique explosive C-4 comes in bricks and would have to be taped to each pillar and set off using an inserted blasting cap and common bell wire and a 9-volt battery and some kind of timing device. It does the job very efficiently, but goes off with a hell of a loud noise, like yelling 'fire in the hole". None of that makes any sense to me. I'd definitely concentrate my attention on each of those large, reinforced concrete pillars that supported the building erected on top of the train station. Now, since we don't know if there is any conspiracy afoot to draw you back to the scene of the destruction as part of an either simple or elaborate scheme to kill you, Air Force One is taking off immediately and flying you to a destination known to me as only a set of map coordinates (to Captain Johnson, only as a compass bearing and distance, assigned altitude and airspeed). Once there, he will receive further instructions from the War Room in the White House from the Chairman of the Joint Chiefs of Staff. Captain Johnson will then brief me. We'll proceed from there as the scenario unfolds and the situation demands. "Mr. President, as

Agent in Charge of your safety, I am now in total control of where we fly and where we land. I will keep you informed as I feel "you need to know". "Now, Sir, just enjoy the ride to wherever." "Oh, yes, one more thing, Sir. Don't be a bit surprised in the aircraft does a "touch and go" at whatever airport, and then pull up and fly on to one or more other Airports or Air Bases. No F-16 fighters have been scrambled since I'm aboard and neither the Aircraft nor the President is in any danger that I'm aware of AND we don't want to attract undue attention to Big Bird. Mr. President, we cannot go back to Andrews, since this might just be an tactic to get you in a vulnerable position. We cannot do anything predictable. Anything we do must be carefully thought-out, well-planned, and perfectly executed. Agent Ruiz confiscated all of the weapons of his Agents and placed them in the custody of Captain Johnson on the Flight Deck. He kept his own sidearm, though moved it another location on his person. He isolated himself in order to formulate his own plan to best protect the President. He did not want to follow in the footsteps of Special Agent Rufus Youngblood who was head of the Presidential Detail when President Kennedy was killed in Dallas in 1963. "Think, think", Ruiz said, audibly to himself. You're not just another cop walking a beat in some City. You have only one charge - one concern -protecting the President of the United States. You have to somehow crawl inside the head of your adversary, not knowing who he or she may be, what evil they may be up to, or what cause they wish to promote. This is what you have been trained to do and you must do it. There is no other choice - no one else to consult. He turned to Agent Stabler and tole him to prepare the Emergency Ejection Module, known as the "cacoon", for occupancy and deployment. He then went to see the President in his Private Quarters. He said, respectfully, yet tersely, "Mr. President, I want you to prepare yourself to depart this aircraft prior to landing, with me as your traveling companion. Do I make myself clear, Sir?" The President was pensive for one brief moment and then responded, "that's your call to make - your decision, and I will do as you say." Then, Ruiz tod the President, "Sir, unfortunately, I cannot tell you more at this time except to say that you will need to dress warmly, since we will land at a relatively high altitude location and there may be snow on the ground. The location is totally secure." Agent then went to the flight deck and told the Captain to contact the Commanding Officer of the Marine Base at Camp Pendleton, California. The General was to prepare to receive a visitor as a Code One at the Marine Corps High Altitude Training Site in the Sierra Nevada Mountains, known, informally to Marines as "Pickle Meadows". Any training being conducted was to continue without regard to the arrival of the visitor. "Get a confirmation on that and tell me immediately. Also, prepare for the deployment of the Emergency Module, to land at the following coordinates. For your own protection, I will not tell you who will be aboard the Module, or if it may be deployed without anyone aboard. That is not your concern" The Captain merely responded, aye-aye, Si, and continued to fly Air Force One. It wasn't long before the Captain summoned Ruiz to the Flight Deck. He had received new instructions from the Chairman of the Joint Chiefs. He was to deliver the President to an Air Force Base hi Colorado where the President would be taken to an underground, nuclear-blast-safe bunker. Ruiz didn't like that plan worth a damn. The President would be too isolated and out of the control of the Presidential Detail. "Mr. President, I refuse to allow you to be trapped in a concrete room hundreds of feet underground, underneath a Mountain in a remote area of Colorado that used to be the control room for launching ICBMs during the Cold War. You and I soon enter the Emergency Ejection Module. It will then be jettisoned from this Aircraft and land at a remote Marine Corps Base in Southern California. We will be met by the Commanding General of the First Marine Air Wing at nearby El Toro Marine Corps Air Station who will be your Host. That, sir, is my decision and it is final Now, let's get you ready to enter the EEM." "Captain Johnson, radio back to the Joint Chiefs that I have personally canceled that Order and taken Command of both the safety of the President and flight instructions to the Pilot of Air Force One. There will be no further Orders taken by anyone aboard the Presidential Aircraft. You will be notified, as soon as possible, after the President is safely on the ground in a secure location. There will be no need for any fighter escorts or intercepts, since you can track Air Force One on radar. That is all. Send it now."

Unknown to Agent Ruiz, the Pentagon, thinking "worst case scenario", and furious that its Orders to Air Force One had been canceled by Special Agent Ruiz, had ordered a B-l Bomber to fly high-level reconnaissance over Air Force One. Also, aC-117 with a Navy Seal Team aboard, and a CH-53 Marine helicopter with a Team of Recon Marines aboard, were both flying just "out of sight" of Air Force One.

Ruiz escorted the President into the EEM, closed the hatch and locked it. Captain Johnson "pressurized" the EEM and ejected it from somewhere on the underside of the Presidential Aircraft. The President was no longer aboard. Agent Marty Stabler, however, WAS still aboard. Something, a minor, but important detail, suddenly occurred to him and he rushed to meet with Captain Johnson on the Flight Deck. Agent Stabler hoped he wasn't too late. "Captain, Sir, with the President no longer aboard, have you changed your Call Sign for any radio transmissions?" "No, why do you ask?" "Well, isn't that Standard Operating Procedure for Air Force One and any US Navy ships as well?" "Yes, but…" Marty cut him short, "Good. For Security reasons, this Bird is still Air Force One and the President is still on board" "Roger that, Sir. By the way, I just got my ass soundly chewed out by an Air Force Four-Star for disregarding a Direct Order from the Chairman of the Joint Chiefs He and they are thoroughly pissed and they let me know about it IN SPADES. First time I EVER heard the 'F' word, even in an encoded transmission." "What the hell's their problem? They know the procedure for the emergency movement of a Code One. Ruiz and I are IN CHARGE on this Aircraft from 'wheels up to touchdown and taxi'." "They KNOW that, Sir, but they are very shall I say "territorial".

They take Orders from nobody but the President - Code One Actual. In the absence of the President, they are King of the Hill. They wear four-stare each and I wear only Eagles. My Orders now are to return this Aircraft and all aboard, directly, non-stop, to Andrews. Since your "Charge" is no longer aboard, just have a seat, relax, and enjoy the ride - you are now just another passenger with a ticket purchased by the Taxpayers."

Three parachutes landed the EEM reasonably gently, on a slight, snow covered slope of land high in the Sierra Nevadas of southeastern California. Shortly before ejecting the EEM, Captain Johnson had experienced a rather strong cross-wind of around 20 knots. He decided to lower his altitude to 20,000 feet. This would lessen the amount of time the EEM would be swaying around under the three parachutes, while allowing ample time for the three parachutes to fully deploy. The Air Force and NASA had learned some nasty lessons from retrieving Space Capsules from the waters of the South Pacific in the days before the Space Shuttle. The Space Capsule had once landed on its side in rather choppy waters. It's speed of descent was much faster when one of its three parachutes failed to fully deploy and it hit the water at a steep angle. It bobbed around in the water for a while, and then began to sink. A powerful CH-53 helicopter had dropped its "retrieval cable and hook" The Frogman assigned to attach the hook to an "O" ring atop the Capsule, was faced with a very tricky situation. The downdraft from the helos blades caused the large hook to "dance around in the air", being whipped by the thirty feet of cable hanging from the winch of the helo. On the first two tries to snap the hook onto the O-ring, the hook violently jerked away. On the third attempt, the attachment was successful. However, by then, the Capsule was deeper under the water and full of water itself. When the door (hatch) was opened from the outside, by Navy Frogmen, a large wave "broke" against the side with the open hatch and nearly drowned the Astronauts inside. The Astronauts had barely escaped the deluge, but the flooded Capsule began to sink below the surface of the Ocean. Then three events had occurred almost simultaneously. The steel strands of the braided, one-inch winch cable were starting to separate and fray which would quickly snap the cable. The motor for the winch had nearly reached total weight capacity and was audibly straining. The engine on the CH-53 was very close to "red-lining". To the pilot, that meant to get his external load jerked free of the water and airborne, or tell his Winchman, through his headset to literally cut the cable. He had, maybe, 30 seconds to decide. Then, the pilot decided on a different strategy. He'd turn his helo into the wind and bank sharply, hoping that by dragging the Capsule, instead of a straight deadweight hoist, he'd encounter less resistence to the water. It worked. The Capsule slowly rose in the water and actually began to create a small wake behind it. Suddenly, the Capsule literally "popped free" of the grip of the water and was airborne. He wouldn't try to stabilize his external lift just yet. He'd do that when he hovered over the deck of the Aircraft Carrier waiting nearby. Those thoughts and more, ran through the mind of Captain Johnson although all of that was now out of his control and in the hands of Agent Ruiz. Immediately after ejection, the EEM had assumed the forward airspeed of the aircraft from which it had dropped. That had been about 350 knots. The drag of the three chutes would slow that to about 25 MPH as the EEM actually landed on terra firma. BUT, what if the EEM had, instead, slammed into the rocky side of a mountain and then tumbled onto some slope. The EEM was designed to take that sort of punishment, BUT the President and Ruiz would get a headache out of the bouncing around that they would not soon forget. As it would turn out, the Captain had worried himself over possible situations would never occur.

Agent Ruiz opened the hatch and stepped out into a few inches of powdery snow. He was followed by President Cameron. Shortly, a jeep drove up with Marine Brigadier General (one-Star) Wayne T. (Tom) Adams riding shotgun. General Adams was Commanding Officer of the First Marine Corps Air Wing at El Toro, near the sprawling Marine Base of Camp Joseph A. Pendleton, Home of the First Marine Division. General Adams, a Naval Aviator, was about 6' tall, 185 pounds, with a square jaw and a low voice. He had served a Combat Tour of Duty in Vietnam in 1967-68 as a Captain. He had risen, steadily through the Officer Ranks, alternately serving Tours with Flight Squadrons and Air Support Squadrons. He welcomed the President, first by saluting and then with a firm handshake. President Cameron was about 6' tall, 190 pounds and pretty much in-shape. He shook Ruiz's hand, Ruiz being about 5' 10" and 175 pounds - almost all of it muscle, and commented, "you must be the Special Agent in Charge of the Presidential Detail aboard Air Force One. Nice to meet you." It was obvious to Agent Ruiz that the General had been well-briefed on the overall situation. A second jeep with only a driver had pulled up directly behind the jeep carrying the General. Immediately, a Master Sergeant and a Gunnery Sergeant who had been riding in the back of the General's jeep, jumped out and took seats in the second jeep - the Master Sergeant now riding shotgun and the "Gunny", alone in the rear seat, directly behind the driver. The General motioned for the President to take the shotgun seat up front next to the driver. He hopped into the back seat right behind the President and motioned Agent Ruiz to take the other back seat directly behind the driver. Then, almost as if it had been carefully planned and choreographed, the sky above them was filled with parachutes as elements of Navy Seals and Recon Marines landed nearby. General Adams wryly commented, "well, we have ourselves quite a show here, don't we? I was told this was 'top secret stuff, which is why I'm up here in a jeep and not a "six-by" truck. Jeeps, I can get all day long with just a phone call from my Chief-of-Staff. Getting a damned truck means explaining things to the MTO (Motor Transport Officer) about why I need it and where it is going and when it will be back in his Motor Pool. How are all of these paratroops going to get off this Mountain top, anyway ?" "Ruiz- to- General: "Begging your pardon, Sir, that's your problem and no concern of ours. I did not either Order them or ask for them. Their presence is the work of the Chairman of the Joint Chiefs of Staff. He got 'em here - he can get 'em outta here. Can we get out of here, now, General, Sir ? You bet, Agent Ruiz - hit the damned gas, driver, and hand me your radio. "Colonel, Adams, here. Send two CH-53's up to Pickle Meadows, ASAP. They are to pick up a Team of Navy Seals and a Team of Recon Marines who've just completed a secret training exercise. That is all. Adams out!" Then, Ruiz yelled to the General, "damn I like your style, Sir. Keep it up and maybe, just maybe, you'll be Commandant." A quick "Roger that, came, in unison, from the Master Sergeant and the Gunnery Sergeant from the trailing jeep." The General had the last words - "what are you waiting for, Corporal. Didn't you hear me tell you to hit the GODDAMNED gas?" "Aye, aye, Sir."

RETURNING TO THE SEAT OF POWER

The next morning, Special Agent Ruiz and President Cameron were aboard an airplane assigned to the Commandant of the Marine Corps for a direct flight to Andrews Air Force Base. Upon landing, they were taken by helicopter Marine One to the South Lawn of the White House. Agent Ruiz was met by the Director of the FBI and Vice President Paul Jacobs and told to "take some time off", along with Special Agent Stabler. The President went directly to the Oval Office. He called in his entire National Security Team. They were waiting outside his Office for instructions from his Chief-of-Staff. He ushered them into the Oval Office. The President began, "here is what I know. The Pan Am Building in New York City is now a pile of rubble, sitting atop the trains of Grand Central Terminal. That's it. That is all I know. First, I want an estimate of those killed and those injured. Next, has anyone or any group claimed responsibility for this ? Third, our best guess as to whether this was the work of some deranged person, some political group with a particular cause, or some organized terrorist group, such as we cannot assume it and neither can we rule it out Al Qaeda. First, the Director of Homeland Security. "Mr. President, at this point in time, we have nothing - no clue. The building just collapsed.". "Okay, next, the Director of the National Transportation Safety Board. What do you know, if anything?" "Sir, nothing definitive, so far, Sir. Nobody or Group has claimed responsibility. There is a lot of rubble, a lot of things and people crushed under tremendous weight. No apparent explosions, no particularly loud sounds from eyewitnesses. Just a sort of subtle shaking, like, maybe, a small earthquake. Then, the PanAm building just came straight down and crumbled under its own weight into a huge pile of debris - concrete, dust, twisted steel and aluminum, plaster and glass. That's it, Mr. President, Sir, that's all I know to tell you. Anything else that I might add would be pure speculation on my part and I'm not going to go there." "Well, I see the Vice President sitting over there looking none too pleased. What's on your mind, Paul? "Well, Mr. President, where do you want me to begin. No, scratch that. I am angry, unhappy…. no, royally pissed.

Here we sit, the brains of this Administration. Yet nobody has a clue as to why the Pan Am Building has ceased to exist? C'mon, everybody, let's get real. Nobody here knows shit from shinola about this tragedy? I don't happen to believe that. If it is true, then all of us should have asked the President to be excused while we go try to find out what happened. There is another, not-so-little matter, Mr. President, that I find really, especially galling. It has to do with you leaving Air Force One hi 'emergency mode' some goddamned where over the Rocky Mountains. Now, Sir, I don't have any real problem with that. It was a decision made by the Head of the PD, charged with protecting you. He had little information to go on and wanted you in a secure area, on the ground. That was not a bad call, from where I sit. However, what is this crap about the Joint chiefs of Staff wanting to send you into a damned underground bunker under a Mountain somewhere in Colorado? You'd be isolated and without comm. If the bad guys ever found out where you were hiding, they's just wait you out and then kill your ass. MREs and bottled water don't last forever. Who gave the JCS power or permission to make that decision? You, the President, are their boss and all of the time, they knew exactly where you were. Flying in their damned Airplane. You mean to tell me that JCS can't get on the horn to you aboard Air Force One, explain the situation and ask you where it is, on the ground, from which you would like to continue to carry out the duties of your Office? Doesn't JCS you have any control over your destiny?" "Mr. Vice President, I am the Air Force Member of the Joint Chiefs. I made the suggestion to the Chairman of the JCS that we make the decision of where to place the President on the ground and to communicate that information ONLY to Captain Johnson, the Pilot of the Presidential Aircraft. Captain Johnson disregarded a direct Order from the Chairman by telling Special Agent Ruiz of our Order and allowing Agent Ruiz to disregard it. I, and we, on the Joint Chiefs, consider that action to be a Court-Martial Offense and we intend to prosecute it under the Uniform Code of Military Justice (the UCMJ). We cannot stand idly-by, while one Special Agent of the FBI and Secret Service, decides that he knows better than we do, when he is 30,000 feet in the air and five of his Superiors have our eyes and ears tuned to not just the United States, but the entire World. That, Mr. Vice President, is my, and our, defense of our situation and subsequent action, in a nutshell, sir." "Well, General, I think that just sucks - it just plain sucks -is that plain enough for you, General?" "I'm sorry you feel that way, Mr. Vice President, Sir." "Well, I do, General. Furthermore, with the President's approval, if you should pursue a General Court against Captain Johnson, as is your right, I will personally arrange for your Retirement, after your demotion to Colonel.. That is, AFTER your immediate Resignation from the Joint Chiefs. Call it a 'quid-pro-quo' if you wish. Revenge is a nasty word I don't like to use. Think about that, General. " The President had heard enough and finally spoke up "I'm the guy you're all talking about. I think the JCS may have 'jumped the gun' a bit here and overreacted. Pilot Johnson did the right thing in informing Agent Ruiz. Ruiz was correct in overriding Orders from the JCS. I'm the only one who can do that and I was standing right next to Ruiz when HE did it. I'm still alive and safe and life goes on. General, tell your fellow Generals what I just told you and there will be no Court-Martial of Captain Johnson. Paul, the next time you have an outburst like that, be sitting in my Chair, as President. We're done here. Now, let's go out into the cruel world and see what we can find out about why there is no longer a Pan Am Building in New York City. We are finished here. All I want to see right now is rear ends heading out the door."

ALQAEDA GOES HIGH-TECH

New York Fire Chief, Anthony Carmine Rizzo stood next to Vice President Paul Jacobs, looking at the wreckage and total devastation of what had been the Pan American Building. It had been something of a marvel of structural Engineering. With no more land available in Midtown Manhattan, it was decided to build something atop something that already existed. Grand Central Station was the site of choice. It stood on nearly a full City Block. The Terminal, itself was sunken a full story below ground level. It was full of wooden benches of folk either waiting to board trains or waiting to greet and pick-up arriving passengers. Two large Information Booths were located on the floor. It had a high-vaulted ceiling, full of glass-paned windows that allowed long rays of light in the morning. These shafts of light splashed circles of light on the tiled floor. This is where you waited for the PA to announce either the arrival of a train, or the beginning of the boarding for the train you may have been waiting for to take you to either Long Island, or "points North". Trains for New Jersey or points West, were serviced by Pennsylvania Station, partway across town. What distinguished Grand Central was its extremely high Cathedral ceiling in the waiting area,

In the mid-to-late 1960s, Pan American World Airways bought the "Air Rights" to build on top of Grand Central Station. The construction left the Terminal almost completely intact, huge waiting area and windows, included. The construction went deep into the "track area", below the Terminal, jack-hammering just enough of each concrete floor and drilling below the train tracks into the bedrock of Manhattan, to install five-foot square, steel-reinforced, concrete pillars. Enough such pillars to support the modern, multi-storied Pan Am Building, with a helicopter landing pad on its top. THAT, in its entirety, was what had suddenly come crashing down into one huge pile of rubble. The real cause for immediate concern was that it had happened at the start of evening commuter rush hour when hundreds of thousands of daily commuters were heading back to their homes in the suburbs. At that hour, trains run every 10 to15 minutes for at least two hours, starting at about 4:59 until about 7:23 PM. Each train is about ten cars with about 50 passengers per car. Normally, each car is full. Some trains include a "bar car" at the rear where commuters can have a cocktail or two on the ride home and pay cash for it. Some of those cars, presumed to have been in the "kill zone" could have the injured or killed figured to within about 10% accuracy. The only "gross passenger count" you could not determine was the number of passengers who bought tickets on the train. You would not know that until the Conductor turned in his receipts the next day. To complicate matters, all of the trains heading North into Westchester County and on into Connecticut to Hartford, traveled through underground tunnels from Grand Central at 42nd Street, to 125m Street where the tunnels ended and the trains surfaced onto Elevated tracks, stopping at 125th Steeet as the last stop before they crossed the Harlem River at Hells Gate and entered the Bronx. There was no way of knowing how many, if any, of those trains' passengers were subjected to asphyxiating, or choking fumes and dust from the falling debris that may have entered the tunnels and been sucked along by the rapidly exiting trains.

It was quickly determined by Chief Rizzo and his team, that the cause of the catastrophe had to be centered around some or all of those concrete supporting pillars. He had already consulted an Expert in Implosion Demolitions by Contract. There was no question but that the pillars failure was the sole cause of the collapse of the building. Now to determine just how. The "why" would wait for later. The train cars' fates and the condition of the passengers within would have to wait. There were piles, hundreds of feet high that would have to be carefully removed before getting down to the level of the tracks and the train cars. It would take weeks, maybe even months. It occurred to Chief Rizzo that this IS the actual definition of "terrorism" -the fear of the unknown and the probably "yet-to-come". To make you feel unsafe, anywhere, anytime, all of the time. To cause you loss of sleep, appetite, and energy. To make you just want to give in to the bad guys and give up living. Wasn't THAT, the ultimate goal?

Out of nowhere, there came a possible break in the case. A boy, age 9, had been waiting, on his bike, at a traffic light at Grand Central Station and 42nd Street. His new AM/FM radio, a birthday gift from his parents, fastened to his handle-bars had literally exploded. He got off his bike and picked up all of the pieces and put them in his pocket. "Bummer", he thought. He went home and told his parents what had happened. His father took the pieces to the store where he had bought the radio. The technician was puzzled, but asked if, by chance, his son had been listening to FM radio? "That's all he listens to, as far as I know. Why?" "Well, sir, the FM receiver part has really been fried. It's been subjected to a signal surge that I've never seen before. We'll be glad to give you a replacement at no cost to you, but I'd like to keep this one, if you don't mind." "Its all yours, I have no need for it."

The technician went to a party that night. He and a few others were talking "techie talk" and he mentioned the fried FM radio the kid's father had brought in to him. "Any idea what would or could cause that?" "Yeah, said one guy. You ever been around a High School right when school gets out? The kids with the expensive sound systems in their cars like to crank up the volume of the bass. At over 200 amps, it is below the hearing range of the human ear, but it will make your ears vibrate and you have to cover your ears with your hands or you'll get a real nasty headache. At over 300 amps, the vibration will easily crack or flat-out break the windows in nearby houses. It will also cause dog's and cat's ears to bleed. Some Rock Concerts can pump out 500 amps. If you're more than 500 yards from the sound stage with the amplifier, the vibrations diminish a little, but the smoke from the marijuana and the alcohol from the beer make up for it and you get one hell of a high - it's a real trip, dude !"

The next day, the Technician looked up the name of the Customer who had returned his son's radio because of the fried FM circuit, in his Sales Data Base from his Register. He called the Customer. "Sir, you recently returned your son's radio with a fried FM receiver?" "Yes, I did, and you replaced it at no cost. My son really enjoys it when he is riding his bike. Is there a reason you are calling me now?" "Yes. Where did you say your son was when his radio broke -did you say at the corner of Grand Central and 42nd Street?" "Yes, that's where he was." "That's all I wanted to know, Sir. Thank you very much."

"Hello, I need to speak to the FBI Agent-in-Charge. It's very important. It has to do with the collapse of the Pan Am Building, recently. I don't want to get involved, but if I were you, I'd be looking for any Radio Station anywhere close to the Pam Am Building with the capability of broadcasting an FM radio signal with 500 Watts of power. Then I'd check their logs to see who was on Duty at the Control Panel at around the time the Pan Am Building collapsed. That is all I will say. The rest is up to you. Goodbye."

Ordinarily, the FBI would have "poo-pooed" such information as coming from an unconfirmed and, therefore, unreliable source. However, in the Pan Am case, they had absolutely no information, other than the obvious pile of rubble, and no leads. On a hunch, the FBI Agent called Fire Chief Rizzo to report what the caller had said. Rizzo didn't "toss off" the information. He called the Demolition Engineer. Could there be a connection between a very high amperage FM radio signal and any weakening of the re-barred concrete pillars supporting the Pan Am Building ? "Interesting question, replied the Engineer. At this point, anything's possible. Vibration has been know to compromise the stability of concrete. I remember a case a while back in a hotel lobby. There was a concrete walkway, above the lobby, suspended from the ceiling by steel rods. That's called a "flying bridge". Anyway, a rock band was playing in the hotel lobby that night. People were standing on the concrete walkway, beers in hand, leaning over and listening to the music of the band. There were several jaunty tunes being played and the amperage was relatively low, but the folks on the walkway began to dance among themselves on the five-foot wide concrete walkway, supported only be those steel rods hanging from the ceiling. The steady movement of maybe 50 pairs of feet on the four-inch thick concrete walkway caused it to begin to undulate and the vibration caused chips of concrete to begin to flake off from the slab. In the revelry, nobody took any particular notice until larger pieces of concrete began to fall and hit some of the dancers on the floor below, eliciting more than a few "ouches". Then, the entire concrete-slab walkway crumbled and collapsed, sending everyone on it crashing onto the floor below. There were many injuries and a few fatalities. Chief, what's the source of the information, or do you know?" "Well it apparently came from a Technician at a radio store who sold an AM/FM radio to a man to attach to the handlebars of his son's bike. The kid was waiting for the light to change at 42nd Street and Grand Central Station. Suddenly his FM Station went dead and the radio fell apart. The kid picked up the pieces and his Dad took them back to the store for a replacement radio. The Technician told his Dad and later reported to the FBI that the FM receiver was totally "fried", was the term he used. The Demolition Engineer began to put all the little pieces of information together in his head. Could it be? Could it happen ? Yes it COULD happen. It may, in fact, have happened and caused the Building to collapse and fall straight down on top of the tracks. Chief, have one of your men bring me any small section of any concrete pillar two to three feet long. I'll need to examine it closely." "You got it, Sir." "Chief, in my line of work, we do the exact same thing, except we wrap each pillar with a band of C-4 plastique explosive, insert a blasting cap, and run bell wire to a central signal receiver, such as a Cell Phone's battery. We buy one of those disposable Cell Phones and pay for the minimum number of pre-paid minutes. It doesn't take much juice to set off a blasting cap. We tie the pillars together with steel cables to make sure that none falls to the outside of the building. Obviously you can't do that unnoticed with such as the Pan Am Building. Then you just dial the Cell Phone number and hit the Send button. C-4 bricks of explosive duct-taped to each pillar does the rest. There's a very real possibility that a relatively small FM radio receiver, set to a non-Commercially-assigned frequency, could be attached to several key pillars. Take out those pillars and the remaining ones cannot support the load of the Building and it would all come crashing down. Send a signal to each of those receivers, all tuned to the same frequency, at the same time at, say, 300 Watts of power. Then, coordinate that with the scheduled time of the departure of the maximum number of trains all leaving at about the same time, vibrating along the rails. I'll bet you'll find many tiny cracks in the sections of pillars you can quickly retrieve. Once the steel rebar is not held firmly in place by the crumbling concrete around it, it will bend easily and further crack the concrete for about a foot on either side of the bent portion. Also, at the time the Pan Am Building was erected, it was common for rebar to be delivered to the site early and just pulled off the flatbed truck to lay on the ground for a while. Rain and humidity took their toll on the steel rods just strewn on the ground. Mild oxidation (common rust) begins to set in. The same thing happens to us humans who get sunburned- The sunburned skin slowly flakes or peels off. The difference with the rebar is that the tiny flakes of rusted steel are not regenerated as happens with human skin. It's not much of a loss of steel, but multiply that over hundreds of steel rods and there is a potentially weakening effect. That doesn't happen these days, since the rebar is delivered to the site in large bundles and is picked up by cranes and placed under some kind of cover for at least a little protection against the rain and weather elements. Chief, since we have nothing else to go on right now, let's embrace the "vibration theory". Get a list of all FM radio stations within, say, a mile of this site, that broadcast or have the capability of broadcasting with up to 500 Watts of power. Then check their Logs to find out who was controlling the output wattage from, say, Noon of the day of the collapse until the actual collapse. Then, have the FBI and Homeland Security run a background check on each of those people. If, and only if, Al Qaeda is responsible, I'll bet you'll find an area "cell" with one or more "sleeper" Operatives involved. Don't forget, Chief, if it IS Al Qaeda, they are Zealots, not crazies or stupid. They are not "druggies" or drunks. They are working toward their Cause and they truly believe in their Cause. Let me know what you find out and we'll go from there. We don't need any wild speculation or unfounded assumptions from the Political World, so let's keep this strictly to ourselves. Even the President doesn't need to know. Stay in close touch with me and get me a section of a pillar as soon as you can. Talk to you later, Chief Rizzo."

BITS AND PIECES

President Cameron paid a visit to the site of the former Pan Am Building. Air Force One flew into nearby Floyd Bennett Field . The President had with him, his Secretary of Transportation, Secretary of Homeland Security, Head of the National Transportation Safety Board, Special Agents Ruiz and Stabler and their Detail. They were met by New York City's Mayor, Fire Chief Rizzo, the District's City Councilmember, the District's State Assemblyman, Congressional Representative, both New York's US Senators, and the Governor. They were split up among Marine One Helicopter, Marine One-Alpha, and Marine One-Bravo which had flown up, empty, from Quantico, Virginia. They were flown to a helipad next to Pier on the East River and taken by motorcade to what had been the Pan Am Building.

Chief Rizzo's radio went off and he excused himself to take the call privately. He received some good news. He returned with it to publicly brief the President and all of the gathered Elected Officials and Dignitaries at an informal and impromptu News Conference. The President didn't seem to mind the "public" briefing. If he did mind, he said nothing to anybody about it. Chief Rizzo began, "local Railroad Investigators had been able to determine at about what time the last commuter train had either passed or stopped at the 125th Street Station. The two tracks Northbound accounted for both the Local trains and the Express trains. Given the time of the building's collapse, the exact time of departure of each scheduled train (to within 30 seconds), the average speed of each departing train, and the known distance from the Terminal to the 125a Street Station, they were able to calculate how many train cars had been trapped somewhere in the tunnels. It wasn't nearly as many as had first been feared. That was the good news. It had been decided to have rescue people enter the tunnels from 125th Street, riding two-person motor scooters which could squeeze between train cars and the walls of the tunnel. They could also ride over small piles of debris. We will have no "handle", at all, on the number of train cars damaged or crushed, or casualties or fatalities, until our Rescue Personnel do a car-by-car, seat-by-seat inspection. We can't go by the calls we receive from wives looking for missing husbands, either. Businessmen often miss their intended train and take a later one. They may still be at their Offices. Those who came after the collapse have really no alternative but to pay for an expensive ride in a taxi. Some cabs refuse to drive way out into the suburbs. There was more good news. Chief Rizzo got a report from the leader of the Motor Scooters riding inside the train tunnels. There are apparently no fatalities and few serious injuries - just cuts and scratches from broken train-car windows. There is a First-Aid kit in each car that has enough antiseptic and small bandages to handle most of the minor cuts. The Crews have arrived at the cars directly under the Pan Am Building. Some train cars have partially-caved-in roofs, but nothing below the backs of the car seats. Some of the falling steel fell at an angle that lodged them in the side walls of the tunnel and effectively formed a barrier to prevent more debris from hitting the tops of the train cars. They are lodged, m-place, pretty firmly and will have to be cut out with torches. THAT IS good news. Our best guess is maybe a couple of hundred passengers needing rescuing. None appear to have broken bones or other serious injuries. All appear to be lucid and responding well to questions from their fellow passengers. Completely against the "odds", we have not come across one MD among any of the trapped passengers. We've gotten plenty of bottled water to them and a few have even asked for a cold beer, That's the Big Apple for you. We've now got about two hundred Motor Scooters and small motorcycles, each ferrying one passenger at a time out of the tunnels to 125th Street for either treatment or trains to take them home. They've got a kind of a "Conga line" set up where they enter the tunnel southbound along the right side of the cars, cross the track between trains, pick up their one passenger, and drive back out of the tunnel to the North along the other side of the cars. I'm told the round trip takes about 20 minutes due to the slow speed required in the narrow space between each car and the concrete walls of the tunnels and the only light being the small headlight of the Motor Scooter. Each passenger must hug the torso of the driver and remember to keep their feet and legs as close as they can to sides of the Scooter. The Scooters get about 30 miles to the gallon of gas and have about a three-gallon gas tank capacity. We should have all passengers out of the tunnels by early tonight. Then we can start searching through the rubble from the actual, collapsed Pan Am Building, itself, picking through it piece-by-piece, just as we did with the Twin Towers of the WTC some years ago. That ends my part of this Conference. Mr. President, do you wish to add anything else, Sir?" "No Chief, I have nothing else to add. You're "on top of the situation" here. My entourage will only get in your way by encouraging folks to ask you a lot of questions to which you do not have any answers. They'll want some sort of a "edge" for the local television News. You and your folks don't have the time to be messing with that. I will now be returning to Washington. Thank you all for coming out, today. That is all."

Chief Rizzo managed to grab Special Agent Stabler before he got on the helicopter for the short flight to Floyd Bennett Field. The Chief asked Agent Stabler to try to have Agent Ruiz to arrange a private meeting with the President aboard Air Force One, before it departed. Agent Stabler contacted Agent Ruiz who "collared" the President, who agreed to the meeting. "What is it, Chief? What's on your mind". "Mr. President, there's something I think you should know. I have become aware of some information that I think bears on this situation. It may, on its face, sound like something straight out of Science Fiction, but I have this "gut feeling" that it may be true. I have consulted with a Structural Engineer who does "building implosions" under contract to the owners of buildings. Most of his work involves older buildings which have been "tax depreciated" to their maximum. He razes them to create room for new construction or Parking Lots. He "drops" large buildings, under Contract to their Owners, for a fee. What he does, legally, is exactly what somebody has done, illegally, to the Pan Am Building, I do believe. He uses the plastique explosive C-4. It comes in the form of a brick bat and is rather malleable.. Attach it to something structurally-weight-supporting and with your finger, push a blasting cap into it. Then run its two tiny wires to a power source, such as a 9-Volt battery inside a "Hell-box" detonator, give the handle one firm twist of your hand to generate a small jolt of electro-magnetic power, and "up goes whatever". HE hooks his blasting-cap wires to a disposable Cell Phone, then dials the number, hits the Send button and "up goes whatever".

This Engineer tell me that there is a form of "demolition" known, informally, as "vibration induction". It has to do with the transmission of very high wattages of radio amplification, using Frerquency Modulation (FM). Three to Five Hundred Watts of amplified power sent to an FM radio receiver attached to structural concrete, is enough to cause small cracks in the concrete and compromise its "structural strength and integrity. Can you see where I am going with this, Sir? "I think so, but go on - continue." "I" have much more detail I can give you on this, but this is not the time, nor the place. I just wanted you to know all that I know and now I have done that. Agents Ruiz and Stabler know how to contact me if you'd like me to give you all of the details that I am aware of. That's all I have for you, Mr. President. I'll take my leave of you now. Have a nice day, Sir." "Wait a minute, Chief. In your opinion, do you think there is any connection with Al Qaida here?" "I'd be willing to bet on it, Sir." "Oh, and why is that?" "Mr. President, I think Al Qaida has gone "high tech". They used brute force and sacrificed half a dozen of their best Operatives on the WTC Mission. They tried once to blow up those towers with rented Vans filled with explosives from the underground parking garage. The basic technique wasn't outright damage to the garage. It was "vibration and echo" to destabilize the supporting concrete pillars and columns. Then allow the sheer weight of the building, people walking around on each floor and the movement of the many elevators, do the rest. They'd have done it, too, except the blast was not powerful enough. They just miscalculated and used nitro instead of fertilizer. Some American malcontent copycats went the fertilizer route and blew the hell out of the Alfred Murrah Federal Building in Oklahoma City. That DID work It just wasn't Al Qaida. When AlQaeda failed with the blast from the trucks in the underground garage, they got their ego involved and resorted to using commercial Airliners as manned rockets. THAT was expensive in the loss of life on BOTH sides, but, BY GOD, they DID bring down both Towers, which was their goal. Now, I've got my Structural Engineer ready to closely examine any piece of any supporting column that my Firemen can find and deliver to him. He'll check it out for any signs of cracks, flaking, separation or crumbling that was caused by "vibration and echo". Then, he'll test an in-tact piece using an FM radio receiving 300 to 5oo watts of power transmission amperage from some commercial radio transmitter. I'll give it a couple of days to a week until we know something definitive. We can then rule out that theory or start looking for a Licensed Radio Station with that capability that was "on the air and actually transmitting an FM signal" at about the time of the Building collapse. I've already asked the FBI to ask Homeland Security to check out all of those Stations, find out who the on-Duty Engineer or Technician was and do a detailed background check on all of those who meet that criteria. That is my full brief to you, Mr. President. Any questions, Sir?" "None at this time, Chief. Just keep me closely informed Your contact with me will be through Agents Ruiz or Stabler directly. That way, you can eliminate being asked a lot of stupid questions from my Staff trying to impress me. Gotta get back to the White House, now, Chief. Thanks for all of your hard work and keep me fully informed. That is all." "Roger that, Sir."

Back at the White House, the President immediately called a meeting of his entire Cabinet. He began, "I've just been to what WAS the Pan Am Building in New York. FAA is not a part of this. NTSB, FBI, Homeland Security, and the FCC will be heavily involved. New York Fire Chief Anthony Rizzo is very much on top of the situation. It appears we will be dealing with a somewhat technical term of "vibration echo". Any of you ever heard of that term? I guessed you had not. Now, I don't want to see any of you taking notes. I want your full and undivided attention. I want you listening to me with BOTH ears and concentrating on what I have to say. Nobody takes a sip of their coffee or scratches, wherever. I am NOT ruling ANYTHING OR ANYONE, OR ANY GROUP out, period. However, THAT having been said, there are some subtle indications that this may have been the work of Al Qaeda. Chief Rizzo briefed me in considerable detail aboard Air Force One before we lifted off from Floyd Bennett Field in New York City. The Chief has neither prejudices, nor preconceptions. He deals only in known quantities of known quality. He leaves no stones unturned, as it were. We do know this much. There was no explosion of any kind before the Pan am building fell - not so much as a cap pistol or a firecracker. .There were no warnings ahead of time and no phone calls after-the-fact, claiming responsibility. What we are apparently dealing with here is what I shall call 'one cool customer' The odds favor an operation of an Al Qaeda Agent, but, so far, that has NOT been proven - just a hunch or a somewhat-educated guess. I do know this much - at about the time of the Incident, someone's portable FM radio, very close to the site, was rendered inoperable, as in totally fried, by a very high wattage FM radio transmission- Sound Engineers have told Chief Rizzo that the FM signal had to come from a reasonably near-by Commercially-licensed Radio Station capable of transmitting between 300 and 500 watts of power. That's where you come in, Mr. Federal Communications Commission. I want you to get with Chief Rizzo to find out what Radio Stations, within about a mile of the Pan Am site, could have that capability. Now, I don't give a damn what power transmission they are Licensed for. Do an on-site inspection with technicians trained and experienced in determining such a capability. First, get a Federal Court Order to search the Station and take a couple of Federal Marshalls with you. Touch base with the Federal Courts and the Chief of Police in New York City before you do so. Fm told your guys should be 'in and out' in less than hour unless there is some equipment hidden and you have to tear down a wall to get to it and check it out. Try not to tear up an entire Radio Station. You must have meters or some instruments that will tell you what electronics are inside a wall. Oh, also inform the Mayor of New York of what you will be doing. And you guys with the Search Warrants, try tact and diplomacy with the Radio Stations I well remember when former US Attorney General Robert Kennedy used to personally lead his 'troops' raids on Union Offices in New York back in the 1960s. They'd shout 'raid-raid" and bust down the door with wooden rams so nobody inside had any time to hide anything (they didn't have paper shredders in those days). We don't need to be doing any of that sort of crap. Chief Rizzo has already asked Homeland Security to 'stand-by7 to do a thorough 'BP (Background Investigation) on all technicians who may have been on-duty for any Radio Station with a high-wattage FM radio transmission capability in the vicinity of the Pan Am Building. We may be dealing here with a sound phenomenon known as "vibration-echo". What the hell is that, you ask. Well the best way I can explain it is, have you ever been around a car, likely driven by a teenager, with the bass kicked-up on his or her car stereo. It's that very low "boom-boom" sound. It drives dogs and cats nutso and can make their ears actually bleed, since it breaks their eardrums. It is below the range of human hearing, but will give you a nasty headache very quickly. If the car stops, it can crack or break nearby house windows. The vibration actually cracks the glass. Then the sound bounces off an interior wall of the house and breaks the glass on the rebound. The technical term for it is "vibration-echo". Now, 50 or 100 watts of radio power output is just a nuisance. However, 300 to 500 watts of amperage output can cause even rebarred concrete to chip, crack and crumble. Chief Rizzo and I think that may be the cause of the building collapse. The Chief has a Demolition Structural Engineer checking out a chunk of a column for any sign or evidence of 'vibration-echo1. He'll let me know as soon as he finishes his testing. Relatively few train cars were trapped in the rubble. Those who were trapped reported relatively minor injuries - cuts and scrapes - no broken bones, and apparently no heart attacks. All passengers are safely home, now, as far as I know. This concludes my briefing to you. Isn't THAT an interesting turn of Events -I'm briefing all of you, instead of the other way around. Hmm, that's interesting. Now go and carry out your respective duties. That is all - you are dismissed - get gone. Chat among yourselves on YOUR time and not mine."

CHIEF RIZZO'S REPORT

The President's Chief of Staff entered the Oval Office. The President was sitting at his desk. "Mr. President, New York Fire Chief in on line one for you, Sir. The President picked up line 1. "Good to hear from you Chief. Got any news for me?" "Yes Sir. My Demolition Structural Engineer has finished his examination of several pieces of the fallen reinforced concrete columns. He has found definite evidence of "vibration-echo" in at least three different sections of the support columns/pillars. Cracks and small chipping of the surface concrete were found. Some crumbling was found around some rebar rods. As you may be aware, Sir, concrete, as opposed to sand mortar, has pebbles mixed in with it. Vibration-echo causes the sand mortar to separate from the pebbles, ever so slightly. The sand mortar does not adhere well to the pebbles naturally since both are of a different chemical composition. What makes them adhere is pressure and compression supplied by the steel forms that surround the columns until the water has evaporated and the mix is relatively 'cured-out'. So-called 'green concrete' is a term for concrete that still contains a good bit of moisture within it. While it may be somewhat dry to the touch of a finger-tip, the head of a hammer would disappear into it. Those who pour concrete regularly and deal, daily with tall columns, will not pour another section of column on top of a section that has not cured-out, at least enough to remove the steel casings from the last section poured. There was no problem found with that part of the concrete-pouring process. However, when the Engineer just tapped a column-piece with a common nail hammer, the pebbles came popping out from the mortar that should have held them in place. That is one of the classic signs of "vibration-echo", I'm told. Mr. President, I think we now know what caused the Pan Am Building to collapse. It would be my suggestion that we now turn our attention to finding the source of the culprit FM Radio Station that transmitted the high wattage/amperage signal. If it was Al Qaeda and if I know anything about Al Qaeda, the Radio Station will not be complicit and will have no knowledge of its possible involvement. The scheduled Engineer or technician may have called in sick, legitimately, and would have found a replacement on his/her own -'opportunity and desire' then may have presented themselves to a terrorist. That what 'sleepers' and their cells are all about and that's why they exist. The Russians did it commonly during the days of the Cold War. They had 'sleeper' Agents of the KGB that were actually Citizens of this Country until they died without ever being 'activated and used'. Former Soviet Ambassador to the US, Anatoly Dobrynin told, after the fall of the Soviet Union inl991, of several 'sleeper KGB Agents' who were never activated'. Mr. President, I recommend STRONGLY, that we proceed very slowly and deliberately, based on the little information we have. No Federal Storm Troopers with Search Warrants, just now. We've got a pretty good handle on what caused the actual collapse, Who actually pushed the buttons or threw the switches to set it all in motion is quite another question. THAT question is very much unanswered at this time. Sir, let CAUTION be the Rule until you have enough irrefutable and definitive information to conclusively prove otherwise." "I quite agree, Chief. Thanks for the info and the call. Stay in touch.? "You can bet on it, Mr. President. Good Day, Sir."

President Cameron immediately called his Attorney-General. He told the AG, "I just heard from Fire Chief Rizzo. He's 99% sure the Pam Am Building collapsed from a "sound phenomenon known as 'vibration echo' ". It's when a very strong FM radio signal is broadcast in the direction of things made of, or supported by, concrete. The radio signal tends to make the concrete crack and crumble. To do any damage to concrete, the signal has to be a minimum of 300 watts and, more likely, 500 watts. In case you didn't know, 500 watts is a shitload of broadcasting power, or so I am told. I don't know crap about any of this, but Chief Rizzo and his consulting Demolition Structural Engineer do. I want your forces to call upon, NOT 'raid' every Licensed Radio Station within a mile or so of the Pan Am Building. Have your Search Warrants in-hand and ready to serve, but DO NOT SERVE THEM unless you are denied entry by either a Station Employee or the Station Manager him or herself. There are to be no Storm Trooper or Gestapo-like tactics used. Do you understand and do I make myself absolutely clear ? You are not Bobby Kennedy, using the 'Carte Blanche' of his brother, the President, to strong-arm people to get their attention and force their compliance with profanity-laden threats. I have every reason to believe that your Agents will be able to gain entry into each Station by a simple knock on the door and flip of a Federal Identification Badge. You're to look at no files. The limit of your Warrants is to find legitimate transmitting equipment that may have been tampered with to boost power output enough to reach the 3 00 to 5 00 of amplification output. You'll have sound technicians with who have the equipment needed to make that determination. I'm told than none of the transmitting equipment is small enough to have been easily taken to the Station and then removed. In all likelihood, nobody at the Station was aware of anything different having been done. Keep that in the back of your mind. For God's sake, don't "piss anybody off" by questioning their honesty in response to your questions. Also, expect a lot of local television coverage. If you should be visited by TV Cable Reporter Bernard Shaw, treat him with great respect. He's well known in New York, liked and respected. That is all.

A line of gray Government Sedans began to emerge from the underground parking garage at the New York Federal Building. They were unmistakable with their 'GS, Tax Exempt" License tags. The line of them, each with four people, fanned-out across Midtown Manhattan, heading to different, assigned, Radio Stations. The Federal Marshalls visited every Radio Station for which they had a Search Warrant. They were Official, yet polite and never had to actually 'serve' any of their Warrants. They turned up nothing unusual.. One Station's Chief Engineer told them that to boost an FM signal, the equipment required COULD be carried in an ordinary athletic gym bag. A simple pair of 'alligator clips' clamped to existing equipment in the right place, could do the job and would be nearly impossible to detect, after-the-fact. You'd have to know exactly where the jaws of the clips were clamped onto existing wiring in order to bite through the insulation and make solid with the insulated wire. The tiny holes made by the penetrating teeth of the clips would be almost impossible to detect to the human eye. Another Engineer disagreed. For that much of a boost in output," someone would need much larger clips and stronger clamps. Like car-battery jumper cables. AND, the clamps would have to be attached where the wires (or cables) attached directly to the terminals on whatever equipment had been used. Any other method or configuration would fry the wires if any clips were attached directly to them. We're talking wires no bigger around than maybe a round toothpick leading into the actual transmitter. The wires COULD have been as big around as a soda straw. Any appreciable boost in power applied to the transmitter would have had to be applied by some sort of large, metal clamp directly to the electrical terminal of the transmitter, itself. It's kind of like jump starting your car's dead battery. You clamp-on the jumper cables over top of the cables already there, apply the jump, start the car, and then disconnect the jumper cables. Even a forensics expert, using sophistocated equipment, could not tell you that jumper cables had definitely been clamped onto the battery terminals." Both Station Engineers agreed that there was no definitive way, at this time, of telling which Radio Station's transmission equipment may have been misused or tampered-with. The Radio Station Manager did offer one piece of advice to the Marshalls. "I'd be checking Station Log Books to see who was the Engineer or Technician on-Duty during the time-frame you need to know about. Any call-ins or substitutions? Any Visitors not properly logged-in? If it were me, I think I'd even dust for fingerprints. All of those of our Staff and Employees are on file with the FCC with a copy in our Personnel files, right here in the Office. You're welcome to photograph them, but not to remove them from the Station Office." "Mr. Manager, one Marshall chimed in, this Federal Warrant give us the right to remove anything we want from your Office." "Mr Marshall, Sir, I also know that the Federal Communications Commissions has placed certain requirements upon us that we dare not violate if we wish to keep our Operating License and remain on-the-air. I have no idea whose regulations and requirements take precedence - do you?" "Not exactly, Sir, but if I had to place a bet on it, I'd go with a Search Warrant signed and issued by a Federal District Court Judge. I think even Vegas would place bets on the Federal Judge's Warrant to trump and Rules of the FCC." "Okay, okay, Mr Marshall, you win, for now. Take the fingerprint cards you want or need, but sign the receipt for them with my Secretary - I've gotta cover my ass, I'm sure you understand." "No problemo, Senor - muchas gracias, and hasta la Vista, baby, as Telly Savalas said in the movie 'Cannonball Run" with Burt Reynolds, Frank

Sinatra, and Dom DeLuise. See ya, Senor. But before my men leave, we'll dust for fingerprints on and around your transmitter." "As you wish, Sir - help yourself - do your 'thing'.

Now to report back to both the AG and Chief Rizzo. The fingerprints taken from the transmitter matched those on the Station's fingerprint cards, except for one set. It matched prints on FBI files for one Ibrahim Salaam Ibrahim, an Iranian National, on an extended Visa for Computer and Engineering Studies at New York University in Manhattan. A check with the University Chair for those Departments turned up spotty attendance at Classes with no Degree awarded. The "Bureau" checked on his local address, an apartment in the Bronx. He had been on a month-to month lease arrangement, always paying in cash, and had checked out and vacated the apartment on the day AFTER the collapse of the Pan Am Building. He had then flown out of JFK, using his real name and valid American Passport, on a direct flight to Berlin, Germany. From there he had taken a flight to Budapest, Hungary and on to Prague in the Czech Republic. Then on to Rome, Italy, and finally to Paris, France. Why such an indirect route using his valid American Passport? He had no dual Citizenship anywhere. Maybe he wanted to avoid suspicion by being so open in his travels. Maybe, maybe, maybe, whatever. The FBI had enough evidence, it thought, to go to a Federal Grand Jury for an indictment. The "charged" man would never show up in Court to defend himself. His Court-appointed Attorney would plead either 'not guilty to all charges', or 'no contest" (nolo contendere). The Court would accept the plea, whatever it was, find the Defendant guilty of Contempt of Court, in absentia, for failure to appear in Court, and set a date for a Trial that would never, actually, be held. The 'accused' would never be able to exercise his Constitutional right to confront his accuser (the US Department of Justice for the Federal crime of, basically, multiple, anonymous, premeditated homicides). The Court-appointed Defense Attorney would inform the Judge that he had been unable to locate his client to bring him to Court. In all likelihood, the Defense would NEVER be able to bring his client to the court. Therefore, the Prosecution would rest its case based on a positive match of the Defendant's finger prints found on the transmitter that sent the signal that caused the supports of the Pan Am building to collapse. Unable to rebut, the Defense would rest its Case. The Judge would render "summary Judgment" in the maximum penalty allowed by Law, and adjourn the Court. The Judge would inform the Defense that should the Defendant EVER return to the jurisdiction of the District Attorney for the Borough of Manhattan, he would face immediate arrest, forfeiture of US Passport, and incarceration until his set trial date. His Court-appointed Attorney was his Attorney-of-record, and would continue to be if the Defendant EVER returned to the jurisdiction of US Federal Courts, anywhere in the United States. Extradition from anywhere in the US was handled on an individual-state basis. With many foreign Countries, extradition was possible according to Treaty with individual Countries. Within the United States, there was no Statute of Limitations on Mass Murder. There certainly was no limit on the prosecution of those who had any part in Hitler's Holocaust. Crimes against humanity will be hunted down and those responsible in any way will be held accountable to the full extent of the applicable law(s) at the time of capture/arrest. That was the US Attorney General's 'read' on the whole situation and he so-advised President Cameron. So far, there were no dead bodies found in the trapped railroad cars. There probably would be some found, trapped in the rubble of the collapsed Pan Am Building. That would bring to bear the charge of homocide. The Motive would fall under the new Federal Statute of TERRORISM. The third legal element required for prosecution of the case, 'a person (or persons) charged', would be identified to the Court, legally, as one or more "John or Jane Does". The weapon would be "(sound) vibration-echo" from a high-powered radio transmission. At this point, it really didn't matter who the person or persons responsible were or whether they had any affiliation with Al Qaeda. America had been successfully attacked - AGAIN. Now to wait for the Chief to complete the tedious process of cleaning up the mess. In the process of doing so, we would know the extent of the "human damage". Maybe, also, discover exactly how the concrete pillars were actually weakened and caused to crumble. The President ordered the NTSB to stay on the site in New York until all of the debris had been cleaned up.

CLEANING UP THE MESS

Chief Rizzo supervised the huge and time-consuming process of removing the rubble from what had been the Pan Am Building. They had several huge cranes on-site to remove the many precariously-hanging steel beams. It was a process similar to the game of 'pick-up sticks" you played when you were a kid.. The "sticks", were like foot-long, large, round toothpicks. There were, maybe, thirty-one of them, all different colors. You gathered them into a bundle, which you held together with one hand. Each stick in the bundle stood straight up on its end on a flat surface. You then pulled your hand away and allowed them all to fall randomly in a pile. The idea of the game, was to pick-up each stick, one-by-one, without moving or disturbing any of the other sticks in the pile. Your opponent watched the pile carefully as you removed each stick from the pile. If they detected any movement, whatsoever, to the other sticks in the pile, they had to point to where the movement occurred. You knew if you were 'caught' and you lost your turn to the other player. Sometimes, you had to touch the end of your right and left index fingers to the pointy ends of a stick at the exact same time and remove it from the pile. As you pulled each stick from the pile, you kept it. When the last stick was removed, the winner was determined by who had the most sticks. It had to be an odd number of sticks to begin with since there could be no ties. The Pan Am Building was now one huge game of Pick-up-Sticks, using heavy steel beams. A 'less-than-clean' lift and removal of any beam could cause the whole pile of rubble to move, either horizontally or vertically, or both. The force of gravity would prevail. The "loser" might be someone trapped in the debris, but alive. A careless or hasty lift of a beam could cause injury, greater injury, or death. Since there had been no explosion, there was no fire, and all gas lines had been shut off. However, there was plenty of dust in the air from sheet rock and other sources, so all firefighters had to breathe through plastic masks, with oxygen fed to them through tubes connected to oxygen tanks strapped to their backs. They could not cut any beams, since they could not control how and where the pieces fell. They could not take the time to find the 'balance point' on each beam and attach the lifting cables in the correct place. They could not attach cable hooks to the end of each beam since the few rivet holes where the rivets had snapped off, under pressure, were not large enough for the hooks. It was decided to use electro-magnetic plates, about the size of manhole covers. Since they needed a flat contact between steel beam and magnet, the main crane cable had to hook onto two other cables, each hooked onto the ends of a steel 'spreader bar'. The cables hanging from the ends of the spreader bar, were about 6-feet long and had the electro-magnetic plates (discs) attached to their ends. There was a power line which ran from each magnetic disc to the top of the crane and back down to the cab. A compact, portable, diesel generator had been placed on the rear of the cab, just behind the Operator. There was a distinct 'clank' as each iron disc firmly contacted the steel beam at each end. Then, the 'lift' of the beam was clean, reasonably-level, and even, with no 'dancing around in the air'. Once loaded on a flatbed truck, no time was lost by having crews detach the hooks and cables and ride them up to attach to the next beam.. Once loaded on the truck, the crane Operator just pushed a button in his cab that cut-off the electric power to the magnetized discs. The discs then disconnected from their contact with the beam and were freed to be lifted by the crane to remove the next beam from the top of the pile. And so it went, agonizingly slowly and carefully, from sunup to sundown, until all "structural" material was removed. They could not work at nights, under floodlights, since there would not be enough light. Chief Rizzo's main concern right now, was getting to everybody, trapped, dead or alive, in the pile of rubble Bloodhounds could not be used, since the pile of debris was too unstable even for the relatively light weight of a dog. Bassett Hounds and Shepherds weighed between 70 and 100 pounds. A paw could easily go right through a piece of fallen sheetrock. Rizzo took off his helmet. He was sweating heavily and his short black hair was matted to his head- He was Italian by ancestry (Anthony Carmine "Tony" Rizzo) could be nothing else, but, very obviously, Italian. He stood about 5' 10", and right at 200 pounds. However, with his stocky frame, he carried the weight well and had tremendous upper-body strength, plus a barrel-chest. That came from doing bench presses at the Fire Station on relatively slow days (and there weren't many of THEM). The Chief was feeling REALLY frustrated. He was rapidly running out of time to find and help anyone still trapped in the pile of rubble. What more could he do ? What more could he POSSIBLY do? He hopped up on the bed of one of the trucks partially loaded with damaged steel beams, took off his boots and stretched his toes inside his heavy socks. He opened the hooks holding the top of his protective yellow jacket closed and spread the top wide. He pulled out his tucked-in white undershirt, pretty much soaked in sweat, and pulled it up to his armpits. He fanned the cotton fabric against the light breeze in an attempt to both get some air between it and his chest, and to try to dry it out just a little. He just gazed up at the clear, blue, Manhattan sky as planes were taking off and landing at nearby LaGuardia Airport. Those big metal machines seemed so graceful as they came and went into and from the Big Apple - his City. Suddenly IT came to him. An idea. Could it work? Of course IT could work. Why hadn't he thought of IT before? He gathered himself back together and got on his radio to the head of the Crew of the NTSB overseeing the removal of debris. "Sir, I need to meet with you IMMEDIATELY." "Chief, I'm not at a place where I can make that happen right now. What is it your need?" "Forget it, sir, I'll go another route and get it done another way - thanks, anyway, Sir - Rizzo out".

"Mr. President, Chief Rizzo here. You gave me this number to call you if I had anything new on THE EVENT. Well, Sir, *I* do. I need your help and I need it now. Please, Mr. President, just listen to me. I'm down here, at the site, watching all these men and machines slowly pick apart what's left of the Building. It's KILLING me not to know if there are people trapped and still alive in all of this mess. I think I have a solution to that problem. Could you arrange with the Pentagon to divert one of its "spy satellites" with infra-red capability, to make at least one pass over THE SITE with its high-resolution cameras? Dammit, Sir, if we can read a license plate on the back of a car in Moscow, we SHOULD be able to detect the exact location of sources of heat inside a pile of rubble. That COULD indicate the presence of human beings, would it not? We could then concentrate our rescue efforts in those areas." "Stay on the line, Chief, I'll get it done for you.

I'll have SECDEF open a direct line to your phone immediately. All other frequencies into your phone will be blocked until you tell us otherwise. For practical purposes, your telephone will be dead to all incoming signals except the one used by SECDEF Tell your people to expect their phones to go dead, temporarily. You and they will have to use personal Cell Phones in the interim. You'll know EXACTLY when the satellite has passed over your ACTUAL site and you'll probably be able to wave to the camera. Then we'll send a photo image to the machine in the NYSB van at the site to give you a paper printout, in color. You can take it from there. I'll arrange to keep this line open for you until you advise me otherwise. Keep me advised, Chief." "Will do, Sir, and thanks. Rizzo out." "Chief, NTSB here. Come to our van.

We've got your photos for you " "On my way, NTSB, Rizzo out." "Good to see you, Chief. I regret that it had to be under these circumstances, though. Here's what you wanted. Our guys have given you an actual temperature range for the different shades of color you see. Our reading is that red is still alive at close to 98.6. Pale yellow is barely alive with shallow breathing, poor blood circulation, little pulse and some degree of dehydration. I've contacted your ME and Coroner and they concur in our definitions of body-temperature color. All have been in physical need for up to 96 hours. Brain damage requires personal, physical examination of the victim. You can count the color ranges of the images for yourself and set your own priorities for your rescue Operations. We've done our job. The rest is for you to decide. I'm just damned glad it's not a part of my job to decide which little piece of color to go after first. At least you know, definitively, now, where all of the actual people are located."

From the "supporting members" removed so far, It appeared that the building collapsed at many different angles, rather than 'pancaking' straight down - one concrete slab directly on top of another with a crushingly, devastating, and fatal result. Past experience had shown that such a result had created many 'pockets of survival' - some large enough for an adult to stand up in. Depending on proximity to what had been the outside walls of the building, it's possible that breathing air would have been available to those trapped for quite some time. Their only need would be some kind of nutrition and drinkable liquid. Rizzo now knew where all of the people were. Even a corpse, less than a week old, would emit a very pale yellow on satellite imagery. Given what the crane Operators had told him about the odd angles of the fallen steel beams, they seemed to have lodged themselves where they had fallen, just like the beams that had fallen onto the walls of the train tunnels, far below and under the Building. Chief Rizzo had decided to stop considering the why-fors and what-ifs. Dammit, he now knew where all of the people were in the building. He had good reason to believe that what was left of the building would collapse no further and would simply have to be dismantled, piece-by-piece. He decided to send in, in full force, the firemen, dogs, EMTs, and other Rescue Professional and Volunteers. Time was now their most immediate enemy, not danger from the unstable Building. The work went fast and well. Within a day, it was finished. The dogs had found every 'image' on the satellite map. None was "pronounced dead" on the spot. Several showed signs of having been thrown around the room, incurring minor cuts and bruises. The blood from the cuts had long since clotted. Blunt force trauma to the head had rendered them unconscious. Then Mother Nature had taken over and sent them into a deep sleep, but short of a coma. Their body had gone on "auto pilot", conserving both the body's need for and use of fluids, and the need for solid nutrition. There was no loss of limbs and no evidence of heavy bleeding. All of the victims were taken to the hospital and most, in time, recovered completely. A few had experienced varying degrees of brain concussion. Their recovery would take longer and might never be complete. All-in-all, Chief Rizzo was satisfied with the overall result. It could have been a lot worse - much worse - very much worse, The Pan Am Building had been totally destroyed. Would it ever be rebuilt? He had no idea, nor did he really care. He was, basically, a simple Fireman - not a Real Estate Developer or Builder. The tracks of Grand Central Terminal would be restored to full operation in a week, or so. The "wrap-up" WAS, one building destroyed, one train terminal with service temporarily disrupted. All-in-all, no immediate fatalities, a few serious injuries, lots of minor injuries. Whoever did it had failed in his/her ultimate mission. The trains would run again, on their normal schedule. No doubt, another building would be built atop the Terminal. The space was there. It was available for the payment of "Air Rights" only. The location was nothing short of outstanding- Yes, thought Fire Chief Tony Rizzo, someone WOULD build, again, atop the Grand Central Terminal. It was just a matter of time. He sent his Final Report to President Cameron. The President replied, "Well done, Chief, well done".

A few days later, a message was broadcast from the Television Station Al Jazeera, based in the Middle East. It was pro-Arab and anti-West and was a regular conduit for messages from Ai Qaeda and/or Osama bin Laden, himself. The message was meant for the Unites States and its President Cameron. The message was terse and succinct: "Dear Mr President. 'Gotcha', AGAIN!"